SCARED TO DEATH

Scared to Death

Jahnna N. Malcolm

AN
APPLE
PAPERBACK

SCHOLASTIC INC.
New York Toronto London Auckland Sydney

ISBN 0-590-55217-1

12 11 10   7   6 7 8 9/9 0/0

Printed in the U.S.A.   40

For Maile:
This could have happened to you!

Prologue

Elliot, Muffie, and Quentin were three truly rotten kids. Everyone said so. Their teachers, their parents, their friends, and most of all — their baby-sitters. In fact, a baby-sitter never sat twice for the Bullock family. Sometimes, the sitter would phone Mr. and Mrs. Bullock at the restaurant where they'd be having dinner and announce, "I'm giving you twenty minutes to get back here. Then I'm leaving." Sometimes the sitter would just walk out without even calling. Those kids were that rotten.

This story is about the summer Elliot, Muffie, and Quentin stopped being rotten and started being scared. Scared for their very lives . . .

1

"**O**utta my way, snotface!" Elliot Bullock barked at his older brother Quentin as he made his way to the elevator of the Clifton Towers apartment building in New York City.

"Snotface?" Twelve-year-old Quentin shoved his wirerimmed glasses up on his freckled face. "That's really original. I'm wounded to the core — *lard butt.*"

"What's going on out here?"

A tall, dark-haired man in a trench coat glared at them from the door to their apartment. The pudgy fifth-grader with the straight brown hair and the thin pale boy with glasses chose to ignore their father's question. Their nine-year-old sister answered for them.

"Quentin and Elliot are fighting again, Daddy. It is *so* tedious." Muffie Bullock stood by the elevator door, primly dressed in a floral print frock with white stockings and simple black flats, impatiently watching the dial.

Reginald Bullock III stepped out into the hall

and put his hands on his hips. "I have just about had it with all three of you!"

"Me?" Muffie gasped in shock. "What did I do?"

"You are a whining tattletale," he informed her. Mr. Bullock pressed his hands to his forehead and murmured under his breath, "I don't know how we are going to endure an entire month together in Maine."

Quentin overheard his father's remark and sniffed, "The same way you do every vacation. You hire a nanny and go play golf."

"Is that supposed to make me feel guilty?" Mr. Bullock demanded. "Because it doesn't. I work quite hard to pay for your exclusive private schools. And the few weeks we spend together in December and during the summer, you children manage to turn into a living hell."

Muffie's lower lip started to quiver. "That's not a very nice thing to say, Daddy," she pouted.

Mr. Bullock ran his hand through his hair. "I'm sorry, but sometimes you children are not very nice."

The elevator arrived, and Mr. Bullock and the three children stepped inside. They rode the twelve floors down to Fifth Avenue in silence. When the elevator doors opened in the lobby, they were met by Mrs. Bullock, looking cool and collected in a crisp white linen suit with a matching straw hat.

"Well, children," their mother announced brightly, "the doorman has put your luggage in

4

the van." She narrowed her eyes slightly at Quentin. "Believe me, it was quite a job getting your three bags in the back. I thought we all agreed to travel light this summer."

Quentin blinked somberly at his mother through the thick lenses of his glasses. "You know I never go anywhere without my lab equipment and specimens."

"Specimens?" Muffie repeated. "You didn't bring along those stuffed rats, did you? Oh, gross!"

Quentin Bullock was a science nut. Mr. and Mrs. Bullock couldn't quite figure out where he got this from, since neither of them had any interest in science whatsoever.

Quentin's specific interest was in taxidermy. He had pinned stuffed bats and field mice of all sizes above his bed. His prize effort was the great horned owl that he had found on the highway and preserved in an attacking position, its wings outstretched, its beak open wide as if ready to tear apart its victim.

"It's not gross," Quentin replied. "It's my work. And if you don't like it, that's tough."

Elliot dug into the pocket of his travel bag, pulled out a half-melted chocolate bar, and shoved it in his mouth. "I don't understand why Quentin gets to bring three bags of road kill, and I only get one suitcase."

"Because you only need one, piggy," Muffie replied. "Mother, Elliot's eating again! He's stuffing his face with tons of chocolate."

Jenny Bullock pressed her fingers against her temples and rubbed them in a circle. Her headache was back. Not just one of her average, everyday migraines but *the* headache — the horrible throbbing one she always got whenever the children returned from school. She took a deep breath and tried to force a pleasant smile. It looked more like bared teeth.

"Children." Her voice had a clenched sound to it, like a rubber band ready to snap. "We are just about to start our family vacation. One that we hope will be lots of fun. Let's try to be nice to one another."

She pushed a strand of her dark hair off her face, smoothing it into the pearl clip at the base of her neck. "Because if you aren't nice, this eight-hour drive to Maine upon which we are about to embark will be absolute, total misery. And I will not be responsible for any drastic action your father or I may be forced to take."

Quentin looked at Muffie and the two of them rolled their eyes at the sky.

The large gray van the Bullocks had leased for their trip was double-parked in front of the apartment building. As Mrs. Bullock swung open the sliding door she added, "By the way, Elliot, your sister is right. Not only will that chocolate go straight to your ample tummy but it will ruin your complexion."

"Too late," Quentin chortled as he hopped into

the backseat of the van. "Two zits just popped out on Elliot's nose."

Elliot quickly raised his hand to his face, smearing chocolate across his cheek. That caused Quentin to double over with laughter, which prompted Elliot to punch him hard on the arm, and Muffie to wail, "Mother! They're fighting again!"

Mr. Bullock tipped the doorman, shoved the children into the van, and got behind the wheel. It wasn't the tension in his voice that shut up the children, however. It was the information in the announcement he gave them. "First we're picking up Lucille Andrews at Fordham Road, and then it's on to Maine."

" 'Lucille' is the nanny's name?" Muffie wrinkled her nose. "That is so *gauche*."

Mrs. Bullock spun in her seat. "Now don't start! Lucille is a very nice young lady. I interviewed her and she's anxious to meet you kids."

For the first time since they had gotten up that morning, the Bullock children didn't argue. Instead, a whisper of a smile passed between them. It was their unspoken agreement that, when it came to sitters, they always stuck together.

"We're anxious to meet her, too," Quentin said, pushing his glasses up on his nose with a determined shove.

The traffic out of Manhattan was fierce, but a half hour later the Bullock's shiny van pulled in front of Lucille Andrews' apartment building in the Bronx. A wan girl, with dishwater blonde hair hanging limply against her collar, stood in front of the security gate. She clutched a faded blue suitcase in her hands.

As Quentin watched the girl shuffle nervously to the van, he whispered to his brother and sister, "Piece of cake."

Elliot nodded. "She won't make it to Connecticut."

Muffie tossed a shiny lock of her long, sand-colored hair over her shoulder and said, "She's too nervous. I give her until Massachusetts. By then she'll have calmed down and realized what she's in for."

"Ten dollars?" Quentin murmured, establishing their bets. Muffie and Elliot nodded agreement as they watched their victim clamber into the van.

"Oh, it's so nice to meet you, Mr. Bullock," the girl said in her slightly nasal voice. "I can't wait to see Maine," she burbled. "Would you believe it? I've never even been to Jersey before."

"That's the opposite direction," Elliot announced cheerfully. Then he added in a whisper, "You idiot."

Meanwhile, Lucille wasn't even aware that Quentin had taken a furry object out of his suitcase and slipped it onto her seat as she sat down.

"Lucille, these are the children." Mrs. Bullock gestured toward the children who sat at attention, the corners of their mouths turned up in anticipation of what was to come. Lucille turned in her seat and that's when she felt it.

"Hi, Muff — " Her voice stopped short. Carefully she slipped her hand under her to see what she had sat on. Mr. Bullock was just entering the Cross-Bronx Expressway when Lucille screamed, a high-pitched wail that seemed to go on forever. "Awwwwkkkkk!"

She tossed the hideous animal in the air and it bounced off the inside roof of the van right into Mr. Bullock's lap. Quentin had fixed the rodent's lips into a permanent sneer that displayed all of its teeth.

"Great Scott!" Mr. Bullock shouted. The shock of seeing the gruesome rat grinning at him from his lap, coupled with Lucille's banshee wail, rattled him so much that he jerked his hands off the wheel in alarm. The van lurched to the right and careened across three lanes of traffic, nearly sideswiping a cab.

"Get it off me!" Lucille squealed hysterically, even though the rat had now fallen on the floor by Mr. Bullock's feet. "Get it off!"

"Lucille!" Mrs. Bullock barked sternly. "Calm down. It's not on you."

"*Quentin!*" Reginald Bullock's bellowing voice drowned all the others as he pulled the van to a stop at the side of the highway. He turned back in his seat and glared at his son. "You have had it!"

Before Quentin could protest, Lucille stood up, hitting her head on the ceiling light. "Ow. I hate rats. I absolutely hate them." She shot Mrs. Bullock a look of betrayal. "You didn't tell me about this."

Mrs. Bullock put her hand on the girl's arm and tried to get her to sit back down. "Taxidermy is just Quentin's hobby. Don't worry, dear, the rats are all dead."

"Uck! That's just as bad." Lucille brushed at her skirt several more times as if she thought the rat were still clinging to her. Then she swung the sliding door open. "I can't take this. I . . . I'm sorry, you're — you'll just have to get someone else, that's all."

Before anyone could say a word, the frightened girl had leapt out of the van with her bag, and was stumbling down the shoulder of the highway back toward Fordham Road. She clutched her suitcase to her chest and glanced back over her shoulder several times, as if she were afraid the Bullock family might follow her.

The silence in the gray van was so thick it felt like the van was filled with pudding. Elliot dug in his pocket for another candy bar and took a big bite. (He always ate when he was nervous. Or scared. Or happy.) Finally he broke the silence by saying, "Wow. That was fast."

Quentin pointed to the big black diver's watch on his wrist and tapped the crystal with his finger. "Four minutes, twenty-three seconds."

Even Muffie's voice was filled with awe. "It's a new world record."

10

2

For the rest of the drive to Maine, Quentin, Elliot, and Muffie kept absolutely quiet. They didn't argue over whose side of the seat the pillow was on, or where the family should stop for lunch. Elliot didn't have to go to the bathroom every twenty minutes and Muffie did not get carsick. Each of them knew that they had pushed their father to the utter limit. They chose instead to bask quietly in the glow of their triumphant rout of Lucille, the nervous nanny.

As the van drove into Bar Harbor, Mrs. Bullock turned to her husband and said, "Well, our plans for going to the Randolphs' tonight are ruined."

"I refuse to believe that," Reg Bullock said grimly. The skin around his mouth was white from pursing his lips tightly for the past eight hours. "This has already been the worst *day* of my life. I'll be damned if I let those children of yours ruin my evening."

Mrs. Bullock chose to ignore the fact that he had referred to the children as hers and hers alone. Instead, she took a deep breath. "Well, what do you propose? We can't very well leave them in a rented house. They'll destroy the place."

Quentin and Elliot exchanged sideways glances, knowing their mother was right.

Mr. Bullock glared at his children in the rear-view mirror. "As soon as we reach the house, I'm calling a sitter service. They *must* have at least one on the island. At any rate — come hell or high water — you and I are going to that party."

Muffie listened to her father's announcement and stared sullenly at the summer houses passing by the window. This vacation was going to be like every other one. Their parents would dump them with someone — *anyone* — and then off they'd go as a twosome, happily enjoying their vacation while she and her brothers were left to their own devices with another dimwitted baby-sitter. It was a glum prospect.

Elliot was the first to spot the green and white mansion that was to be their home for the next month. "There it is!" he cried. "I see the house."

Muffie and Quentin leaned forward in their seats. The house known as Maldemere was perched on a steep cliff overlooking Bar Harbor, which was dotted with white sails and fishing boats. From a distance, it looked like many of the other mansions they had passed on their drive through town. A winding gravel drive lined with weathered maple trees led up to the old home, which was three stories tall. It had soaring gables and even a turret at one corner. A broad, covered porch wrapped impressively around three sides of the house.

The expectant looks on everyone's faces vanished as the van drew closer. It was apparent that the place was sadly in need of repair. There were big ugly spaces in the roof where the shingles had fallen off and exposed the roof boards underneath. The covered veranda was sagging in the middle and looked like it might collapse at any moment.

"Mother, is that a broken window?" Muffie asked as she squinted up at the top floor. "I think it is."

Mrs. Bullock didn't answer, but the look on her face told them this was not what she had expected.

"Look at the porch," Elliot said over his brother's shoulder. "It's falling down. There isn't even a step to get up to it."

"Don't breathe in my face, buffalo breath," Quentin snapped.

"I'm not breathing on you, four eyes," Elliot pouted. "I'm just saying that this place looks like a dump."

Quentin turned to their father. "Elliot's right, Dad. I think you got hosed on this one."

Mrs. Bullock rolled down her window to get the clearest picture possible of the tumbledown mansion. It didn't improve the view at all. "Reg, are you sure this is the right address?" she muttered. "Maybe we took a wrong turn, or something."

Mr. Bullock sat with his shoulders hunched over

the steering wheel, peering miserably at the house. "This is the right address. The realtor said it hadn't been lived in for a while but that it had a great view of the water." He shot his wife a dark look. "You *insisted* that we have a sea view. She also said that, if we wanted it, we should grab it because there wasn't anything left to rent in town."

"Well." Mrs. Bullock's voice was clipped and precise. "As soon as we get inside that — that place, we'll call that woman and I'll give her a piece of my mind."

"What's left of it," Quentin muttered.

"Did I hear a smart remark, Quentin?" Mrs. Bullock demanded.

"No, ma'am," he said, slumping down in the seat.

"Good." Mrs. Bullock threw open her door and stepped onto the gravel. "Then get out of this car, and take your things into the house."

"Mother, you're not serious about staying here, are you?" Muffie whined. She sat with her arms folded, not budging an inch. "It's a wreck."

"Well, what do you suggest we do? Sleep in a tent? Because that's our only alternative." Reginald Bullock shoved open his door and stepped directly into a mud puddle. He looked down at his soaked leather shoes and slammed the van door with a jarring thunk.

"Now get your bags and get out of the car!"

Mr. Bullock's voice rattled harshly in his throat

and his face was an ugly beet-red. The only other time the kids had seen him look and sound this awful was the time they had dropped his briefcase full of contracts out their twelfth-floor window onto bustling Fifth Avenue. That time Mrs. Bullock had been forced to physically hold him back. Otherwise the children were certain that he would have murdered them.

Quentin, Elliot, and Muffie grabbed their suitcases and leapt out of the van, making sure to stay as far away from their father as possible.

"Careful on the porch," Mrs. Bullock warned, just as her foot broke through one of the steps. A run shot up her nylons and she grumbled between clenched teeth, "Someone is going to pay for that."

"Don't worry, darling," Mr. Bullock muttered as he placed the key in the lock. "If anyone gets so much as a scratch from this place, we'll sue. And sue big."

Being a prominent New York lawyer he knew what "big" was. So did his family. It made them all feel a lot better about entering the ramshackle old house. They clustered around the front door as Mr. Bullock pushed it open.

A stale musty smell met them from within and Muffie clamped her nose shut with her fingers. "P-U! That stinks."

"We'll open the windows and spray some air freshener," Mrs. Bullock said.

"And Raid," Elliot added, watching an unusually large insect skitter across the threshold and disappear into a crack in the porch.

The Bullock family stepped into Maldemere and stood clustered together in the middle of the foyer. Quentin was the first to speak. "Well, the inside is in much better shape than the outside, which could easily star in *Nightmare on Elm Street, Part Ten.*"

Directly before them, a huge staircase arched up to the landing on the second floor. To the right of the stairs was the living room and to the left, a small library.

"The furniture looks like ghosts," Elliot said, peering into the large living room. All of the couches and chairs were draped with white sheets.

"That's to protect it from dust," Mrs. Bullock explained, dropping her own bag onto the oriental carpet. "You children get those sheets off the furniture. Let's find out if this place is habitable or not."

The kids jumped at the chance to tear things apart, and ran through each of the downstairs' rooms, ripping off the cover sheets and knocking over chairs and lamps in their enthusiasm.

"Keep an eye out for a phone," their father shouted.

"Are you going to call that agent?" Mrs. Bullock asked as she swiped with a tissue at the mass of cobwebs criss-crossing the banisters. "Because I want to give her a piece of my mind."

"We'll call her tomorrow," Mr. Bullock said as he paced in the living room and sitting room, looking for a phone outlet. "First things first. We've got to find a baby-sitter."

Quentin squatted in a corner, eagerly watching a fat black spider devour a fly through his magnifying glass. "We spend most of the year on our own," he said sourly. "Why do we even have to have a sitter at all?"

"Because I don't trust you," Mr. Bullock retorted. "I don't trust you with this house, as tumbledown as it may be. You'd probably torch it." He slapped his hand across his mouth. "Now I've put ideas in your head."

"Reg, you talk like they're some sort of demons," Mrs. Bullock chided. "They're just children."

"Are you sure about that?" It was clear that the strain of their drive to Maine had pushed Mr. Bullock to the end of his rope.

"They just need a firm hand," his wife replied.

"And that's exactly what I'm going to hire for them." Mr. Bullock found the phone tucked in a tiny alcove by the foot of the stairs. "Aha! Now, where's the phone book?"

Muffie had made a pile in the middle of the floor of all the sheets pulled from the couches. As she was admiring her handiwork, she spotted a slender book sitting all by itself on the side table. "Is this it, Daddy?"

"Yes!" Mr. Bullock snatched the book from his

daughter's hands and flipped it open. The beaming smile that had just appeared on his face promptly disappeared. He turned back to his daughter, his eyes narrowing once more. "What is this? Another one of your pranks?"

"No, Daddy," Muffie answered.

Mr. Bullock waved the thin book in the air. "This phone book is from 1953! What good is this? Find me one that's at least from the past decade."

The children ran around the room, looking on bookshelves, inside the sideboard, and under the cupboards in the kitchen. They found quite a few books but none of them were phone directories.

"This is ridiculous!" Mrs. Bullock huffed. "Let me see that book."

Mrs. Bullock yanked the phone book out of her husband's hand and a piece of paper yellowing with age fell out and fluttered down to the tip of her toes.

Elliot retrieved it and read out loud. "Eternally Yours Sitter Service. Beechwood-5789." He looked confused. "What kind of phone number is that?"

Reginald Bullock snatched up the paper and read it again. Then he lifted his eyes to the ceiling and cried, "It's a miracle."

"But dear, that slip of paper is ancient," Mrs. Bullock said. "That agency probably went out of business ages ago."

"Yeah," Quentin agreed as he examined the slip

of paper with his magnifying glass. "All their sitters are probably now a bunch of stiffs in the Bar Harbor Cemetery."

"I don't care what you think, I'm giving them a call." Reginald Bullock picked up the old black rotary telephone and quickly dialed the number on the faded piece of paper. He waited for a few seconds and then announced in triumph, "It's ringing!"

"I don't believe it," Mrs. Bullock murmured.

After six rings there was a click as someone on the other end of the line picked up the receiver. At that same moment a cool draft passed through the foyer and everyone, including Reginald Bullock, shivered.

"Eternally Yours," the children heard a faint voice intone in Mr. Bullock's ear.

"This is Reginald Bullock III. I need a sitter for this evening," he said. "I know it's short notice but is one available? I'll pay extra." He frowned and clapped his hand over his other ear. "I'm sorry, we appear to have a bad connection. Could you repeat that?"

The children held their breaths hopefully, then let out a sigh of disappointment as their father exclaimed with a grin, "Wonderful! We're leaving at seven. Do I need to pick someone up?"

The reply sounded clearly from the receiver. "That's not necessary. I know how to find you."

"Fine, then," Mr. Bullock said. "We'll see you at seven sharp." After he hung up the phone, he stood for a moment with a quizzical look on his face. "That's odd."

"What's the matter, Reg?" his wife asked.

"The woman said she knew how to find us," he said.

"Yes?"

Mr. Bullock shrugged. "I don't believe I told her our address."

3

Promptly at seven o'clock that evening Mr. and Mrs. Bullock stood in the foyer with their coats on over their evening clothes, ready to leave. Muffie, Elliot, and Quentin sat on the stairs, their chins resting on their hands. All of them watched the front door intently. Nothing happened.

After a long silence Quentin checked his black diver's watch and announced, "She's late."

"Maybe she got lost," Elliot offered.

"You said she forgot to ask for the address."

"Maybe she's not coming," Muffie said, pulling her dress over her knees so that it covered her shoes. She turned to her parents. "You're going to have to miss that party at the Randolphs'."

Mr. Bullock ignored her remark and walked stiff-legged over to the phone. "Where's that phone number?" he shouted. His wife handed it to him and he picked up the phone and dialed. A few seconds later he slammed down the receiver. "That's fine," he muttered. "That's just fine."

"What is it, Reg?" Mrs. Bullock asked.

"This time I got a recording informing me that that number is no longer in service." He threw up his arms. "Either we've stepped into the Twilight Zone, or I'm losing my mind." Before any of the kids could comment, he barked, "And no smart remarks from any of you."

Mrs. Bullock heaved a giant sigh. "I guess that means there's no sitter."

"And you're going to have to spend the evening with us," Elliot said, popping a handful of French fries from dinner into his mouth. Mr. Bullock had driven into Bar Harbor and bought them some fast food fish and chips that only Elliot had found appetizing.

Muffie wrinkled her nose at her brother. "Elliot, you've got tartar sauce on your chin."

"And it looks like snot," Quentin pointed out.

"You should know, mucus brain," Elliot retorted with his mouth full.

Mr. Bullock stared at his three children for a full minute. Finally he turned to his wife and said between clenched teeth, "This party is very important to me. I need this party."

"I understand, Reg — " Mrs. Bullock started to say but her husband interrupted her.

"I say we take our chances," he declared. "Just leave the kids, and go."

"Hurray!" Quentin shouted, leaping to his feet. "We're on our own for a whole evening."

Mr. Bullock spun to look at his children. "That's

right," he said, narrowing his eyes. "You're on your own. But if you so much as harm one splinter of this broken-down excuse of a house, I promise that you will be sent off to boarding school permanently. No summers on the coast, no skiing at Christmas. Do I make myself clear?"

The kids stared at him in astonishment. Twice in the same day he had managed to get that once-in-a-lifetime eyes-bulging-face-blazing-red, steam-about-to-come-out-of-the-ears look.

"Yes, sir," Quentin spoke finally. "Very clear."

"All right, then." Their father moved briskly to the door. "Your mother and I will probably be home late. So don't wait up."

"Children," Mrs. Bullock said in a gentler tone as she tried to soften her husband's threat, "why don't you take this opportunity to settle into your rooms upstairs?"

"I'm not sleeping up there," Muffie replied. "Those rooms give me the creeps."

Mr. Bullock swung the front door open and he said, "Then you can sleep on the couch, but we're staying here and that's final."

The slam of the door echoed through the house and the children were completely alone.

Muffie stomped her foot. "This place is gross. It's dirty and old and icky."

"Yeah," Quentin said, dragging his heavy leather suitcase that he had left downstairs into the middle of the foyer. "It's just perfect for collecting. I've already found several new types of spiders and I haven't even left the house." His eyes lit up. "Hey! I'll bet there are bats here, too."

"Bats!" Muffie shrieked. "Inside?"

"Sure," Quentin said, hurrying toward the stairs. "They probably would have come in through that broken window upstairs."

"You mean they could be in the living room?"

Quentin wiggled his eyebrows. "They could be anywhere."

"Don't leave me," Muffie cried. "I'm going with you."

Elliot dumped the last of the fries into his mouth. They were cold and rubbery, but he swallowed them anyway. "Wait for me. If you're going bat hunting, I want to be there."

"What are you going to do when we find one, garbage mouth?" Quentin asked. "Eat it?"

"No. I'm going to shove it down your throat!" Elliot lunged toward his brother. Even though Elliot was younger, he was nearly a head taller than Quentin and outweighed him by twenty pounds.

"Look out, Quentin!" Muffie shouted. "Elliot's going to sit on you!"

"The blimp will have to catch me first!" Quentin took the stairs two at a time up to the second floor. Then he turned to the right and disappeared into the darkened corridor.

"Wait for me!" Muffie wailed as she hurried after him. Behind her she could hear Elliot huffing and puffing his way up the stairs. When she reached the landing there was no sign of her oldest brother. She felt the wall for the light switch and flicked it up. The wall sconce flickered on, casting a dim light down the hall. It wasn't much, but there was enough light for Muffie to see that the corridor was lined with closed doors. She tiptoed up to the nearest one, her bedroom, and flung it open.

Without thinking, Muffie leapt back, half expecting a huge bat to come flying out at her. When nothing happened, she peaked inside the cozy bedroom. Lace curtains hung on the windows, and the walls were covered with a pretty floral print wallpaper. Her suitcase sat on the edge of the four-poster bed where she'd left it hours earlier.

Still searching for Quentin, Muffie tried the other doors. She found several more bedrooms, a musty linen closet, and a tiny study lined with old books. The last door opened onto a narrow flight of stairs that only went up.

By now Elliot had caught up with her. The two of them peered up the darkened stairwell.

"Where does that lead, do you suppose?" Muffie whispered.

"The attic, I'd bet," Elliot replied. He took a few tentative steps up the narrow passage and stopped. "There's a door at the top. Should I see if it's locked?"

Suddenly Muffie felt her arms prickle with goose bumps. They traveled right up into the roots of her hair and made her scalp tingle. "No. No, Elliot. Don't open it."

Elliot sighed with relief. He was having the same eerie sensation, only his goose bumps were crawling up his spine. He came quickly back down the steps and shut the door, making sure that the latch caught firmly. "I don't think Quentin went up there, anyway."

"Hey, look at this!"

Quentin's voice was coming from inside the bedroom farthest to their right. Muffie and Elliot opened the door and looked in. There was no one there.

"Quentin, where are you?" Elliot shouted.

"In here," the boy's voice shouted from behind another door in the opposite wall.

"I didn't notice that door when I looked in here the first time," Muffie said.

Elliot turned the doorknob. It led to what appeared to be a nursery. The room was decorated in faded wallpaper covered with pink-and-blue teddy bears. An old wooden crib rested against the far wall, with a small trundle bed across from it. Two painted dressers, a changing table, and a large wooden toy box overflowing with worn stuffed animals and old toys took up the rest of the room. Quentin was standing beside an elaborately painted rocking horse.

"This is *très* bizarro," Quentin said, giving the horse a shove with his foot. It creaked back and forth noisily on the wooden floor. "It looks like the people who lived here forgot to take their kids' things when they moved out."

"Maybe the people were in a hurry," Muffie said as she examined the stuffed animals. A fluffy rabbit and a Betsy Wetsy doll lay on a quilt on the small trundle bed. The crib held a worn rattle and a crumpled blanket. A plastic tea set was neatly arranged on a low table by the window. The whole room appeared as if the occupants had just left.

"You don't think someone is still living here, do you?" Muffie whispered.

Quentin shook his head. "This stuff is too old-fashioned." He waved his arm around the room. "There's not a thing from Sesame Street. No Teenage Mutant Ninja Turtles. No Smurfs. Nothing."

"Yeah, but look at this candy." Elliot pointed to a jar of hard candies on the dresser and pounced on it hungrily. "All right." He opened the jar and popped one of the red candies into his mouth. It disintegrated and he spit it out.

"Wow!" Quentin said as he watched his brother wipe the sugary mass off his lips. "That's a first."

"This stuff is ancient," Elliot finally sputtered.

"Well, of course, silly," Muffie replied, holding up a framed piece of embroidery she removed from a hook on the wall. "See? This shows all the children's birthdays. The baby, Jonathan Chase Kensington, was born in 1953."

"The Kensingtons must have been in an awful big hurry to get out of here," Quentin murmured.

"Yeah, they didn't pack any of the children's toys." Muffie gasped as she opened a dresser drawer. "Or clothes."

"Okay." Quentin held out his hands. "This is too weird for words."

"But why — ?" Muffie started to say when Elliot shushed her.

"Wait a minute." He put his fingers to his lips. "Do you hear that?"

"What?" Muffie asked.

"Shut your mouth and listen," Elliot replied.

Rather than argue, Muffie did as she was told. They all did. The three children stood in the middle of the room with their heads cocked, listening.

Creak-creak. Creak-creak.

"There it is!" Elliot hissed.

Creak-creak. Creak-creak.

"I hear it, too," Quentin murmured.

"What do you think it is?" Muffie asked.

Quentin stared up at the ceiling. "It sounds like one of the floorboards upstairs."

"You mean, in the attic?" Elliot asked.

"Maybe it's a mouse, or one of your bats," Muffie whispered.

Quentin shook his head. "It's too regular for that. Listen. It's got a steady rhythm." He spoke along with the sound. "Creak-creak. Creak-creak."

"Should we go see what it is?" Muffie asked.

"No way," Elliot blurted out. "You couldn't pay me to go up those stairs. Besides — " He cocked his head to one side. "I think it's stopped."

The others listened for a few more seconds and Quentin nodded. "You're right." He scratched his chin thoughtfully. "I wonder what that could have been. Maybe there's an open window, or something, blowing in the wind."

They listened again, just for good measure, but the house was still. Suddenly the quiet was broken by a loud, flat, buzzing sound. The three children each leapt a foot off the floor at the same time.

"What was that?" Muffie's eyes were huge.

"I — I don't know," Quentin said, his voice hoarse with fear.

The loud buzz sounded again, and Elliot's face lit up. "The doorbell!"

"Of course," Quentin replied. "Let's see who it is."

The children raced down the hall, delighted to get away from the eerie nursery, the creepy attic stairs, and the strange creaking sound. But halfway down the main staircase, Quentin stopped dead in his tracks. "Oh, no!"

"What?" Muffie howled as she bumped right into her brother's back.

"I bet it's the sitter."

"Now?" Elliot said. "But she's late. Almost half an hour late."

"You said she might have gotten lost," Quentin said. "Remember?"

The doorbell buzzed once more.

"Better answer it," Muffie warned. "Remember

29

what Father said about being sent into exile."

"But that was if we wrecked the house," Elliot objected. "We haven't done anything — yet."

Quentin hesitated. "Wait a minute. If Father found out that the sitter came and we didn't let her in, that would probably qualify as homewrecking." He looked at Muffie and nodded. "We'd better open the door."

The children walked the rest of the way down the stairs and across the rug in the foyer. Just before they reached the front door, a sudden gust of cold air swept through the hall.

"Boy, this is really a drafty house." Muffie suppressed a shiver as she reached for the doorknob. "Well, let's see what she looks like."

Elliot slumped against the wall. "That's right, here goes nothing."

Muffie threw open the front door. She nearly passed out. Standing in front of her was the strangest woman Muffie had ever seen. She wore a long black skirt and black blouse with a high collar. In one hand was a blue umbrella. In the other she clutched a maroon tapestry bag. Her high-topped shoes were huge, with long, pointed toes. But it was their new sitter's face that made the children catch their breaths in alarm.

Thick black eyebrows arched across her forehead. A thin beak of a nose hooked over her mouth toward her sharp chin. Her mouth twisted into what Muffie supposed was a smile.

"Good evening, children."

Her voice was shrill and grating, like fingernails scraped across a blackboard. Then she cackled with laughter and said, "I'm your new baby-sitter."

"Oh, my God!" Quentin gasped. "It's Mary Poppins from hell!"

4

"**W**ell, don't just stand there with your mouths hanging open like horrified fishes. Invite me in!"

Muffie shut her mouth and backed away from the door. Quentin, who hated anyone ordering him around, rushed forward in her place.

"I'm sorry, but we don't know who you are," he said firmly. "And no one steps foot in this house till we find out their name."

"That's right," Elliot said, stepping beside his brother. "Our parents told us never to talk to strangers."

"You've already broken that rule," the witch-faced woman said, brushing them aside with her hand and stepping into the foyer. "Because, as you see, we are already in the midst of a conversation. Not a very pleasant one, mind you, but we are exchanging words all the same."

"Just a minute," Muffie said, finally recovering from the shock of seeing the strange-looking woman. "Nobody invited you in."

"No, they didn't." The woman removed her black gloves and tossed them on the small table by the front door. "And that's very rude. But I'll forgive you — " She turned and trained one baleful green eye on Muffie. "This time."

Quentin motioned his sister to join the boys in a tight huddle. "Do you really think she's a babysitter?" he whispered.

"Whispering is also very rude," the woman remarked as she took off her black cape and hung it on a hanger in the front closet. "If you children don't believe that I'm your sitter, here is my card."

Before they could turn around, a slim white card fluttered down in the middle of their huddle. Elliot picked it up and read out loud, "Ariadne P. Belljar, Eternally Yours Sitter Service."

All three of them turned and eyed the woman, who stood motionless by the stairs, her tapestry bag and umbrella clutched in her hands.

"Air-ree-ad-nee," Muffie repeated, sounding out each syllable and squinching her nose up. "What kind of a name is that?"

"When you squinch your nose up like that, it makes you look positively piggy."

Muffie turned to Quentin and Elliot and huffed, "Talk about rude!"

"I say we push her back out the front door," Elliot whispered. "Hard."

Ariadne poked Elliot in the stomach with the point of her umbrella. "I will not have whispering in my presence. If you have something to say, spit it out."

"Yeow!" Elliot yelped. "That hurt."

"It wouldn't if you weren't such a fat little boy," Ariadne replied. "But we'll soon change all that." She pointed to Elliot's right pants' pocket. "Get that candy bar out of your pocket."

Elliot was so stunned from being called a fat boy by a grown-up that he did what he was told. Then she pointed the tip of the dreaded umbrella at his feet. "M&M's out of that shoe."

How she knew about his secret hiding place Elliot didn't know, but he wasn't about to ask questions now. He dug in the top of his high-top sneakers and produced a crumpled yellow bag.

"That's better." Ariadne smiled — or sneered. It was hard to tell which. Her lips parted just enough to bare her yellow teeth. "Much better. From here on out it's carrot sticks for you."

"Here on out?" Quentin repeated. "We've got news for you. Our parents should be home at any minute. And that will be the end of your baby-sitting days with the Bullocks."

"I wouldn't be so sure about that," Ariadne said with a low chuckle.

Her laugh sent a shiver of dread through the children. The thought of spending even five minutes with this awful woman was too terrible to imagine. Quentin decided to put an end to her visit right then and there. He spun to face the old woman and, using a tactic that usually frightened

34

off other baby-sitters, shrieked at the top of his lungs, "Get out of this house you ugly old hag! You look like the stand-in for the Wicked Witch of the West, and you act like her, too."

"Yeah!" Elliot hurled M&M's in the woman's direction — not hitting her, but getting awfully close. "So why don't you just get on your broomstick, and fly back to where you came from."

Muffie threw herself on the floor, kicking her feet and clenching her hands into fists as she screamed, "I hate you, I hate you, I hate you!"

Usually, their all-out three-kid tantrum sent a baby-sitter running out into the night — or at least to the telephone. But not Ariadne.

"That's more like it," she purred. "I like honesty."

They watched in stunned silence as Ariadne sailed past them into the living room. She looked around her and, taking a deep breath, murmured, "Home, sweet home." Then she settled down comfortably onto the couch.

"There's something very strange about that woman," Quentin whispered.

Elliot nodded. "And I don't like it."

Muffie had gotten up off the rug and was prissily brushing the dust off her dress. "What do we do now?" she demanded. "Just wait until Mother and Father come home?"

"Are you out of your mind?" Quentin hissed. "If we do that, they'll see how strict she is and want her back, and we'll be stuck with her all — "

He shot a quick look over his shoulder to see if Ariadne was listening. The old woman hadn't moved a muscle. Just to be on the safe side, Quentin gestured for the other two to follow him around the corner over by the landing for a conference.

"Don't you see?" Quentin hissed. "If we don't get her out before our parents get home, we'll have to spend our entire summer vacation with her."

Elliot shuddered. "Four weeks of celery and carrot sticks."

"She's an absolute hag," Muffie said. "I'll tell Mother we refuse to have her as a sitter."

"Oh, right." Elliot rolled his eyes. "That's going to make a big difference."

"Quit bickering, you two." Quentin knelt beside his specimen case and started rifling through it. "We've got to come up with a battle plan."

"You mean, we're going to attack her?" Elliot asked hopefully.

"Not with guns and knives, or anything gruesome like that, I hope," Muffie said.

"No." Quentin shoved his glasses up on his nose. "I say we find out her weak spot, and then go for it."

"How are we going to do that?" Muffie demanded.

"We'll talk to her," Quentin replied as he took a lumpy green felt bag out of the suitcase. "Ah, here it is. Come on." He stood up and started to walk toward the living room.

"Oh, gross," Elliot said, hanging back. "I can hardly stand to look at her."

"Look, you saw how scared that sitter in New York got when she saw my rat Selsdon. One look at him and she was marching down the highway." He patted the bag holding the rat. "Let's just start talking and, when the time is right, I'll sneak him out of the bag."

"Okay, but make it quick," Muffie said.

The three children entered the living room and flopped into several overstuffed chairs facing the couch.

"Have you come to your senses?" the old lady asked without looking up. She was focusing all of her attention on a long black scarf that she was knitting. One long skein of yarn rested in her lap and the rest was coiled in the tapestry bag.

"Yes, Miss Belljar," Elliot said, forcing a phony smile.

"Good." The knitting needles clicked in between Ariadne's words. "That makes my job much easier."

"What exactly do you think your job is?" Quentin asked.

"I'm here to take care of you. To turn you into decent human beings."

Elliot snorted. "You're going to do all that in one night?"

"Who said anything about one night?" Ariadne replied. "Remember my card?"

"Eternally Yours," Muffie said softly.

"That's right, Little Miss Muffett," the old woman said. "You can't get rid of me."

"We'll see about that," Quentin muttered under his breath. He reached in his bag and pulled out Selsdon. "Here, Miss Belljar. Look what I found in my suitcase."

She raised one bushy eyebrow and peered over her glasses at the snarling rat Quentin held in his hand. "Is that a . . . a . . . ?" she stammered for the first time since they'd met her. "A rat?"

"You bet."

Ariadne leapt to her feet. "Get it away from me. Get it away!" The old woman licked her lower lip nervously. "There are only two things I can't abide — rats and bats. The only difference between the nasty little creatures is one has wings."

"Selsdon won't hurt you, Miss Belljar." Quentin smiled wickedly at his brother and sister. "Here, catch!" He tossed the stiff rodent at Ariadne, hitting her squarely in the chest. She jumped back and crashed into the end table, which knocked over a lamp, which tumbled to the floor. The light bulb burnt out with a loud pop.

"What are you doing?" the woman screamed. "Stop it at once!"

Quentin chuckled as he dug in his bag for more ammunition. This was his lucky day. He not only had a couple of bats in the bag but quite a few other rodents of various shapes and sizes.

Muffie and Elliot dove for the bag, too. Normally Muffie would never have dreamed of touching Quentin's little stuffed specimens. But this was war, and war made people do strange things. She grabbed a shrew, which was the smallest creature in the sack, and ran toward the baby-sitter.

"Here, Miss Belljar, kiss Fuzzy," Muffie said. "He likes it when people kiss him."

Ariadne was rummaging desperately in her purse for smelling salts. She opened her mouth to protest but only a feeble croaking sound came out. Meanwhile Elliot snuck up behind her silently, his hands hidden behind his back.

"If you don't like Fuzzy, why not try Kermit and Mickey?" he said pleasantly, dropping a bull-frog and a field mouse on Ariadne's head.

"It's in my hair!" she shrieked. Ariadne tried to shake the creatures off by spinning in a circle but the mouse's feet got tangled in the hairpins holding her bun in place, and refused to fall off.

While Muffie continued to press her shrew up to Ariadne's face, Quentin came flying in with the coup de grace.

"I vant to suck your blood!" he chortled as he moved the bat through the air, holding it by its wings as if the bat were flying. While Ariadne swatted at Muffie's shrew with one hand, and tried to disentangle Elliot's mouse from her hair, Quentin pushed the bat right to her neck.

"Ah!" he cried. "Fresh meat!"

Ariadne screamed and, snatching the bat from

Quentin, hurled it toward the wall. Suddenly her eyes rolled up in her head until only the whites showed. Her body jerked several times with wrenching spasms. Then her legs stiffened and she fell backwards into Elliot's arms. He was so surprised that he lost his balance and the two of them tumbled to the floor.

"Get off me!" Elliot huffed from beneath Ariadne's ample bulk. "You're the one who needs carrot sticks. You weigh a ton."

The old lady didn't respond. She lay still with her mouth wide open, her glassy eyes staring up at the ceiling.

"Quentin," Muffie whispered, "something's wrong with that woman. What is it?"

Quentin, who specialized in animals that had expired, looked at her carefully. "I think she just bought the farm."

"What?" Muffie asked, completely mystified.

Quentin shrugged. "She's dead."

"Dead!" Elliot shrieked. "Get her off me."

He shoved with all his might, and the body of Ariadne Belljar rolled sideways onto the floor. Elliot scrambled to his feet and rushed to join his brother and sister.

The woman lay in a lifeless heap, not moving, not breathing, not blinking. The three children formed a tight circle around the limp form.

"She's most definitely dead," Quentin whispered. Then he looked up at his brother and sister and said with awe, "And we killed her."

5

For the next half hour the Bullock children remained frozen in their little circle, staring down at the body of Ariadne Belljar. They kept hoping that somehow Quentin was wrong, that the baby-sitter just had a seizure and would soon wake up. But nothing happened. The more time passed, the more they were certain that they really had frightened the old woman to death.

"What should we do?" Elliot asked finally. "Call a doctor?"

"A doctor couldn't do anything for her," Quentin replied. "She's deader than dead."

"But shouldn't we call one anyway?" Muffie asked in a tiny voice that sounded like a three-year-old. She always got that way when she was scared and wanted to cry.

"Are you kidding?" Quentin snapped. "If we call a doctor, he'll want an ambulance, and then the police will come, and there will be a lot of questions, and Mother and Father will come home and think it was all our fault."

"But it was," Muffie pointed out.

"Yes, but we don't want them to know that, dummy." Quentin quickly went around the room, picking up his stuffed animals and stowing them back in their bag. Then he set the lamp back on the end table that Ariadne had tipped over.

"Are we going to tell them it was an accident?" Elliot asked.

"We're not going to tell them a thing," Quentin said flatly.

"You mean, they'll just come home and find her lying there staring at the ceiling?" Muffie asked.

"Exactly." Quentin snapped his bag shut.

"Quentin, the cheese has definitely slipped off your cracker," Elliot declared. "Don't you think Mother and Father will think something is a *little* strange when they walk in the door and find us sitting here on the couch next to a dead baby-sitter on the floor?"

"We won't just be sitting here," Quentin said with an exasperated sigh. "We'll be upstairs in bed asleep."

"I don't think I'll ever be able to sleep again," Muffie whimpered.

"You two are incredible," Quentin said, shaking his head. "Don't you understand? If we don't make this look like an accident, we'll be packed off to military school so fast it'll make your head swim. And they'll never let us come home. It'll be like a life term in prison."

Muffie and Elliot exchanged worried looks.

They both knew Quentin was right.

"So you want us to act like everything was fine when we went to bed," Elliot said slowly. "And it was *after* we were asleep that Ariadne had her heart attack?"

"Exactly." Quentin folded his arms and faced his brother and sister, a smug smile on his face.

Elliot broke into a wide grin. "That sounds like a good plan to me."

The three of them promptly set to work to make the baby-sitter's death look like an accident.

"Let's put her in that leather chair in the library," Quentin instructed.

"You mean, touch her?" Muffie squinched up her nose.

"Yes, touch her," Quentin repeated. Then he added, "And Ariadne was right. You do look like a pig when you do that with your nose."

Muffie stuck out her tongue at her brother. The boys each grabbed the corpse by the arm and waited for Muffie to pick up her legs. She still hesitated and Elliot snapped, "Come on, we don't have all night, you know."

Looking around, Muffie noticed the stack of folded bedsheets resting on a chair by the walnut sideboard. She grabbed one and wrapped it around the old woman's legs so she wouldn't have to actually come in contact with any part of Ariadne's body.

"Okay, on three," Quentin ordered. "We lift her

off the floor and carry her into the library. One, two — *unnngghhh!*"

The children strained with all their might but only moved the body a few inches. They tried again and this time succeeded in dragging Ariadne across the foyer into the library. Once they got her propped in the armchair, Quentin patted her shoulder and announced, "Ariadne needs a nice scary book."

"Good thinking," Elliot agreed. "One that might frighten her to death."

"Right." Quentin moved to the bookshelves lining the walls and grinned. "Something by Edgar Allan Poe."

"Or Stephen King," Elliot called. Stephen King was his favorite horror novelist.

"Should we put a can of Coke on the table beside her?" Muffie suggested.

Quentin shook his head. "Old ladies like that always drink tea. Go get a cup from the kitchen. Oh, see if you can find a tea bag, too."

Muffie nodded and ran out of the room.

"Don't bother to heat the water," Quentin shouted after her. "It'll be cold by the time Mother and Father get home anyway."

Elliot planted himself in a chair opposite the body and dug in his back pocket for the one candy bar Ariadne had missed. He took a huge bite and whispered, "Look, Quentin, I don't trust Muffie. At the first sign of any pressure with Mother and Father, she'll crack and tell them everything."

Quentin found a dog-eared copy of *The Tell-tale Heart and Other Stories* by Edgar Allan Poe and carefully set it in Ariadne's lap. "I know," he said, pressing the woman's limp hands around the cover of the book. "I'll make her take the oath when she gets back, and then she'll have to keep quiet."

"I could only find some instant tea and this old cracked mug," Muffie called from the foyer.

"Well, bring them in here," Quentin called.

"No, come get them," Muffie replied. "I don't like to look at her eyes."

Elliot shot his older brother a *What-did-I-tell-you?* look and went to collect the tea cup. Some juice from the Big Hunk bar had dribbled out the corner of Elliot's mouth and Muffie said, "Elliot, you are totally disgusting."

As if to prove her point, Elliot opened his mouth to show her the chewed remains of the white taffy and nuts filling his cheeks. "I may be disgusting," he said with a smile, "but you are dead meat if you tell Mother and Father about any of this."

Muffie looked genuinely hurt. She stepped into the room and said to Quentin, "I'd never tell. You know that."

Quentin took the chipped cup from her and placed it on the table beside Ariadne. "I *don't* know that. So just to be on the safe side, I want you to put your hand on your heart."

Muffie lay her palm across her chest and as she did so, Quentin turned to Elliot and said, "You, too. We all have to do it."

The three children solemnly put their hands over their hearts and then chanted in unison:

"Spiders, snakes, and lizard heads;
If I tell, I'll die till I'm dead."

Then they locked pinky fingers, turned in a circle three times, and spat over their right shoulders. When the ritual was over Quentin said, "The oath is taken and the circle is formed, never to be broken."

Elliot and Muffie nodded solemnly.

"Could we leave now?" Muffie whispered. "Just being in the room with that woman makes my skin crawl. I hate the way she stares at us."

"She's not staring at us," Quentin said. "I have her head aimed at the book."

"Not anymore," Elliot murmured uneasily.

Quentin spun around in surprise. If it hadn't been for the fact that he was the oldest and had to keep up the impression of being the most courageous, he would have gasped out loud. He had carefully tilted Ariadne's head forward onto her chest, so she would look as though she had fallen asleep while reading. But now the head was turned a full ninety degrees to the side. Her green, sightless eyes were staring right at them.

"What the . . .?" Quentin mumbled, trying to keep his pounding heart from leaping out of his chest.

"You don't think she's still alive, do you?" Elliot hissed.

Quentin looked into the vacant eyes and shook his head. "No. I must have bumped her as I crossed the room and that caused her head to fall sideways."

"Oh."

Elliot and Muffie seemed to accept that explanation readily enough. Quentin was thankful for that, because he knew for an absolute fact that he had *not* bumped Ariadne. But he also knew that there had to be a logical explanation for her head changing position like that. Old houses often shifted on their foundations over the years. Maybe the hardwood floor had a tilt to it that wasn't noticeable to the naked eye.

Whatever the reason, Quentin knew one thing for certain. He wanted to get out of that library, and fast. "Come on, let's go up to our bedrooms before Mother and Father get home," he said.

The three children left Ariadne Belljar sitting in the library chair, a worn book in her lap, a cold mug of tea beside her, and her head turned toward the door. They hurried up the stairs, anxious to get away from her, but paused when they reached the second floor. No one wanted to admit it, but they were reluctant to go to their bedrooms alone.

Muffie had chosen the room closest to her parents, and closest to the stairs. It had seemed like a great idea at the time, but now it was far too close to the unpleasant sight waiting in the library downstairs.

"Um, would you mind coming and sitting in my room for a little bit?" she asked timidly. "At least until I fall asleep?"

Normally Quentin would have ignored her request, and Elliot would have sneered and called her a baby. But having a dead body in the room below made them all feel a little strange.

"Sure," Quentin said. "But the minute we hear Father's car, we have to leave."

Muffie quickly changed into her nightgown and jumped beneath the quilts on her bed. Quentin took up a position on the old cedar chest by the window while Elliot, who had run to the kitchen for a last minute snack, settled onto the chintz-covered armchair by the dresser, munching an apple. Mrs. Bullock had opened the window that afternoon to air out the bedroom and a cool breeze blew the white gauze curtains into the room. At the foot of the cliff below the house the children could hear the ocean waves slapping in a regular rhythm against the rocky shore.

Muffie hummed a tune in a vain attempt to get the events of the past few hours out of her head. Elliot crunched loudly on his apple. Suddenly Quentin sat forward and said, "What was that?"

Elliot paused in mid-bite. "What was what?"

"That sound."

The Bullock children froze, listening to the night sounds.

"The waves?" Muffie whispered.

"No, no," Quentin said. "That other sound." He pointed at the ceiling. "In this house. Listen, there it is again."

They all heard it now — a faint yet steady noise from somewhere above them.

Creak-creak. Creak-creak.

"That's the same sound we heard before," Muffie said in a hushed voice. "What is it?"

Elliot suddenly lost his appetite and tossed his apple out the open window. "I don't know. But I don't like it." He got up from his chair and hurried over to Muffie's bed.

Creak-creak. Creak-creak.

The sound grew louder. This time Quentin hopped off the cedar chest and edged over to the side of the bed. "I don't really feel like going to my room tonight," he mumbled. "Muffie, you don't mind if I stay here, do you?"

Muffie was relieved to hear her brother's plea. "Please do."

Elliot and Quentin climbed into the big bed beside their sister, their shoes and clothes still on, and all three of them pulled the covers up under their chins. They stared up at the ceiling, wide-eyed, listening to the steady *creak-creak* above their heads. It was in that position that they finally fell asleep.

6

A crack of thunder woke Quentin with a start. He sat bolt upright in the bed. Muffie was still sound alseep beside him but his sudden movement had roused Elliot out of his slumber.

"She's got us!" Elliot bellowed. "She's got us!"

"Quiet, you jerk," Quentin ordered, reaching across his sister and punching Elliot. "Do you want Mother and Father to hear you?"

Elliot blinked several times. It was obvious that he was still half asleep. "I had a terrible dream," he muttered. "All about a baby-sitter who died and . . ." His voice trailed off and his eyes widened. "But it wasn't a dream, was it?"

Quentin shook his head. "No, it wasn't a dream, but it's going to turn into a nightmare if you don't shut up."

By now Muffie was awake, too. She propped herself against the headboard and murmured drowsily, "Did the police come?"

"I don't know." Quentin fumbled for his glasses on the bedside table and then looked at his watch.

"Whoa. It's eight in the morning."

"What?" Elliot's eyes popped wide open. "Where are Mother and Father?"

"I don't get it," Quentin said. "They had to have come home by now."

"That means they had to have found Ariadne," Elliot whispered. A flash of lightning, followed by a rumble of thunder off in the distance, punctuated his sentence.

Muffie clutched her brother's arm. "I didn't hear any sirens, did you?"

Quentin pried his sister's fingers off his arm and got out of bed. "No, I didn't. This is really strange."

Elliot rolled out the other side of the bed. "Do you think they decided to wait till morning to call the hospital?"

"That's not like Father at all," Quentin said with a shake of his head. "He usually makes a big deal of things right away." He tiptoed over to the door. "I'm going to see what's up."

The room lit up with another flash of lightning, and Elliot and Muffie joined their brother before the booming thunder reached them. The storm seemed to be moving closer and closer.

"I'm coming with you," Elliot said.

"Me, too," Muffie added.

None of them wanted to admit that they were still feeling queasy about being left alone — especially in the middle of a thunderstorm.

"Besides," Elliot added, "I'm starved."

There's nothing to eat," Muffie said as Quentin ꞁowly opened the bedroom door. "Except maybe another apple or two."

"Now there you are wrong," boomed a voice from the hall. It so startled them that all three children screamed and clutched each other.

Mr. Bullock greeted his children with a beaming smile. "I've already been to the bakery on the square. We have fresh coffee, juice, and lots of doughnuts downstairs." He looked much more relaxed than he had the day before.

"Father!" Quentin choked. "When did you get home?"

"Oh, around two-thirty in the morning," Reg Bullock called over his shoulder as he trotted back toward the stairs. "Looks like we barely beat the storm. It's really foul outside this morning."

"Was everything okay?" Quentin asked as the children followed their father down the stairs.

"Okay? It was wonderful. Your mother and I hadn't seen the Randolphs in months and, believe me, we *needed* that party."

"We meant, after you got home," Elliot prodded. "Things were okay then?"

"Why shouldn't they have been?" Reg Bullock led his children down the stairs and paused for a fraction of a second by the library door. Quentin squinched his eyes shut waiting for their Father to say, *"Unless you're talking about the baby-sitter you murdered in the library."* But nothing happened.

Reg Bullock continued into the living room, picked up the financial page of a morning paper he had bought in Bar Harbor, and casually gestured to the sideboard. A huge stack of doughnuts and cheese Danishes sat there on a large china platter next to cartons of milk and orange juice. "Here you are, kids. Eat."

Elliot was the only one of the three children who took their father's advice. He dove for the pastries, shoving a jelly roll in his mouth while also clutching a cheese Danish in either hand.

"Where's Mother?" Muffie asked.

"She's in the kitchen pouring the coffee from Styrofoam cups into mugs."

"Is she all right?" Quentin asked.

"Yes, of course." Mr. Bullock lowered his newspaper and peered at his son suspiciously. "Why the sudden concern over our health?"

"I don't know," Quentin said with a casual shrug. "I just thought, after the upset with the baby-sitter and all, you might still be mad."

"Don't mention that sitter," Mr. Bullock snapped, turning back to his paper. "I can't get over that woman telling me she'd be here right away, and then not making an appearance."

The children looked at each other and silently mouthed, "They didn't find the body!" They turned together and looked at the library door, which was slightly ajar. All of them knew that a very dead woman was still sitting in there.

A crack of thunder shook Quentin out of his

numbness. He hurried over to the sideboard and picked up a sweet roll pretending to eat it. Muffie promptly joined him.

"What do we do now?" Elliot demanded.

"Do we tell them that the sitter came?" Muffie asked.

Her lower lip was starting to tremble and Quentin knew that if they didn't do something fast, she might crack and confess everything.

"Yes, I think maybe we should," Quentin turned to his brother. "Elliot, you do it."

"Me?" Elliot suddenly choked on his cheese Danish. He was seized by a full-blown coughing fit and sprayed bits of pastry in every direction.

Mr. Bullock looked at his son and raised an eyebrow. "Is he all right?"

"He's fine, Father," Quentin said as he and Muffie pounded their brother on the back. "A crumb must've gone down the wrong way."

"That'll teach him to eat like there's no tomorrow," their father said, flipping his paper.

Quentin, still beating on Elliot's back whispered, "Maybe we can trick him into going into the library. Then once he finds the body he won't wonder why we didn't tell him that Ariadne showed up." Quentin suddenly turned to face his father and said, "Um, have you checked out the library yet, Father? There are some very cool books in there."

"I looked at it when we first arrived," Mr. Bullock replied.

"But have you seen it today?" Muffie persisted.

"Good morning, children," Mrs. Bullock sang out as she entered from the kitchen, carrying a tray with two cups of coffee upon it. "Did you sleep well? I know your father did. He was snoring so loudly he could have roused the dead."

On the word 'dead,' Elliot started sputtering again and Quentin jabbed him hard in the stomach.

"The children were trying to get me to go into the library," Reg said to his wife.

"It does have wonderful books." Mrs. Bullock pulled one off the coffee table in front of the couch. "I got this one this morning."

"This morning!" all three children gasped at once.

Their shout startled her so much she nearly spilled her coffee. "Well, yes, what's wrong with that?"

"Oh, nothing," Quentin said, frantically trying to remember how visible Ariadne would be from the library door. "Did you turn on the light?"

"Well, of course I did, silly. You can't hunt for a book in the dark."

Quentin gulped loudly.

"What book did you find?" Mr. Bullock asked.

"You won't believe this, but I found a first edition of Edgar Allan Poe stories."

"What?" the children shouted once more.

"Yes, isn't it exciting? It was sitting right on the table by the big leather chair."

That did it. Quentin marched across the hall toward the library. Elliot and Muffie were fast on his heels. He threw open the door and reached for the light switch.

Before he could turn on the light, a flash of lightning crashed above their heads and the room lit up as if it had been hit by a spotlight. Quentin gasped in shock.

The arm chair was exactly where it had been the night before. The cup of cold tea sat on the end table just where they had placed it. But there was no body in sight. The cold corpse of Ariadne Belljar had completely disappeared.

Three voices rose into the air in a scream of total terror.

7

"**C**hildren!" Mrs. Bullock called from the living room. "What's going on in there?"

"Nothing, Mother." Quentin's voice cracked and he cleared his throat loudly. "We — we were just a little startled by the thunder, that's all."

Meanwhile Elliot and Muffie were staring hard at the empty leather chair. It was as though they believed that if they looked hard enough, the body would reappear.

"I swear Ariadne was dead when we left her last night," Quentin muttered.

"She had to be," Elliot hissed. "You saw her eyes. There was no one there."

"Then what happened to her?" Muffie asked quietly.

Another bolt of lightning crackled above them, and booming thunder rattled the wooden walls of Maldemere. It was so close by that the children ducked. Suddenly sheets of rain hit the window, like someone was aiming a garden hose directly at the house. At the same time the air temperature seemed to drop twenty degrees and Elliot shivered from the chill.

"Maybe she was in some sort of coma," he suggested, "and when she woke up she got embarrassed and left."

Muffie nodded vigorously. "I believe that. Then we didn't kill her after all."

Quentin slapped his hand across his sister's mouth. "Don't say that. Father might hear you."

"Who cares if he does?" Elliot spotted his cheese Danish that he'd dropped on the faded oriental carpet. He picked it up and with two flicks of his wrist dusted it off, then popped the whole thing into his mouth. Now that he had discovered he wasn't a murderer, his full appetite had returned. "In fact, I think Father should know that the woman he hired not only showed up late, but left early."

"Right." Muffie smoothed her dress, which was wrinkled from being slept in the night before. "And I'm going to be the first to tell him."

Quentin threw himself in front of the library door. "Just a minute. Until we know for certain that Ariadne Belljar is alive and well, no one tells anyone anything."

Then, in an imitation of his father, he arched one eyebrow and peered at his siblings over his glasses. "Do I make myself clear?"

Elliot rolled his eyes and sighed, "Yes, Quentin. Now will you get out of the way? I'm hungry."

"How could you be hungry?" Muffie demanded

as the three of them stepped back into the hall. "You just inhaled half the breakfast rolls."

"Half!" Elliot protested. "I ate three tiny cheese Danishes. And I didn't inhale them. In fact, I could hardly choke them down."

"Gimme a break, lard butt," Quentin scoffed. "You Hoovered them. And I didn't even eat one."

"Will you three keep it down?" Mr. Bullock complained. "I'm trying to think. I can't stand your constant pick-pick-picking at one another."

"I wasn't picking," Muffie protested as she came back into the dining room. "It was Elliot and Quentin."

"Why do you have to be such a tattletale?" Mrs. Bullock asked, not even looking up from her section of the newspaper. "That's just as irritating as this constant bickering."

Elliot stuck out his tongue at his sister as he reached for the sweet rolls. Quentin was feeling pretty ravenous himself and he stomped hard on his brother's foot.

"Ooowww!" Elliot howled. "I think you broke my toe!"

"That does it!" Mr. Bullock slammed his paper down on the end table. "All three of you may go to your rooms. Now!"

"But I haven't eaten anything," Muffie protested.

"Then grab your food and eat upstairs," her father ordered. "Your mother and I would like to read our papers in peace."

Elliot scooped up several more doughnuts and made his way toward the stairs. "Geek brain stomps on my foot, and I get sent to my room," he muttered. "Not fair."

"Another word out of you, young man, and you're grounded," Mr. Bullock warned.

Elliot stomped up the stairs and down the hall to his room. Once inside he marched over to the bed and flopped backwards onto the brightly patterned wool bedspread. Now that Ariadne was alive, he had nothing to worry about except how to go about finishing his breakfast. Elliot stacked his cache of doughnuts on his stomach and decided to systematically devour them all.

Elliot was just about to bite into one with cherry filling when something caught his eye. A long piece of twine appeared to be dangling from the side of the jelly doughnut. Elliot sat up to examine it closer.

"It's not twine," he said out loud. "It's more rubbery." Elliot figured the bakery must have got some package wrapping caught in their doughnut maker. He tugged on what seemed like a two-inch length of rubber. Then the sides of the doughnut split apart to reveal the most disgusting thing Elliot had ever seen in his life.

"A dead mouse!" he shrieked. "In my food!"

This mouse was not one of Quentin's taxidermy specimens. Its insides were still there. In fact, what Elliot had mistaken for cherry filling was actually mouse guts.

60

Elliot flung the rest of the doughnuts off his lap and hopped around the room, yelling at the top of his lungs, "Gross, gross, *gross!*"

Then he froze in the middle of the room, wide-eyed in horror. He had already eaten several cheese Danishes. Was that really cheese inside them? He couldn't be sure. He hadn't really been paying attention because of all the commotion over Ariadne. Elliot suddenly felt an awful gagging feeling in his throat, like he was going to throw up. What if that yellow goo in the cheese Danish was really some small animal's brains?

"Barf-o-rama!" he choked, clutching his throat. "What kind of a sick goon would play a joke like this?" Elliot straightened up. There was only one person who could answer that question. And Elliot just happened to be related to him.

"*Quentin!*" Elliot bellowed as he burst out of his room and pounded down the hall toward his brother's room. "I'm going to massacre you!"

Quentin didn't hear Elliot — partly because of the pouring rain that was coming down like a waterfall on the house, but mostly because of what he had just found in *his* suitcase.

A slender little snake, ringed with bright bands of color, lay coiled at the bottom of his suitcase, ready to strike. Quentin had been tossing his clothes onto the bed without really looking when the creature's sudden movement had caught his eye. His hand stayed frozen in midair as he tried to figure out what kind of snake this was. Then a little rhyme he had learned in Boy Scouts flashed through his mind.

"Red and black, friend of Jack;
Red and yellow, kill the fellow."

Quentin stared down at the snake and gulped. There was no mistaking the red-and-yellow bands marking the reptile. It was definitely a coral snake — the deadliest snake in North America!

Suddenly Quentin's door flew open and banged against the wall. That distracted the snake just long enough for Quentin to leap backwards out of striking range.

"I'm going to break your scrawny neck," Elliot roared.

Quentin stood on top of the bed, trying to make his mouth form words, but he was too shaken to speak. All he could do was point a shaking finger at the suitcase. Elliot turned just in time to see a shiny snake slither out of the suitcase and disappear under the dresser.

"Get a . . . get a gun!" Quentin gasped.

"A gun?" Elliot bent over from the waist and tried to peer under the dresser. "What for? It's just a harmless garden snake."

"Get back, you idiot," Quentin shouted. "That's a coral snake and it nearly got me."

"Serves you right having one of your specimens turn on you!"

"That's not one of my specimens," Quentin retorted, feeling a little foolish for standing on the bed. He stepped gingerly onto the floor, keeping a careful eye on the dresser. "You know I can't stand snakes. They give me the creeps." He shuddered. "They make my skin crawl."

"How can you like rats, mice, and bats, and not snakes?" Elliot demanded.

"Because they have fur. Snakes don't."

"Well, I hate fur," Elliot roared, remembering the mouse in his doughnut, and why he was in Quentin's room. "Especially fur with guts oozing out of it."

"What are you talking about?" Quentin asked, putting his hands on his hips.

"I'm talking about the mutilated mouse you stuffed in my doughnut."

Quentin made a face. "That's disgusting. I'd never do anything like that."

"Oh, come on!" Elliot exploded. "Muffie couldn't have. Mother hates the little runts, and Father certainly wouldn't have done it so that leaves only one suspect — you!"

"Oh, yeah?" Quentin shot back. "Then I could say the same about you. You know I hate snakes. And you are the only one in the family who likes them. So you're the one who put it in my suitcase." He shook his head in stunned disbelief. "A coral snake. What were you trying to do, kill me?"

"Of course not, moron," Elliot said. "First of all, where would I get a snake like that in New York City?"

Elliot had a point and for a moment Quentin was stumped. But he recovered quickly. "You could have gotten it here," he charged. "It's been raining, and snakes always come out when it rains."

"Oh, yeah, sure!" Elliot said. "This morning while you were asleep I snuck out of bed, went out in the rain, got soaking wet, found a snake that *doesn't even inhabit this part of the country*, put it in your suitcase, and got back in bed. And was instantly dry." He hooted in derision. "What a genius."

"Well, the disgusting creature didn't just crawl in there itself," Quentin bellowed. "Somebody had to put it there."

"I think *you* did it," Elliot charged. "To freak everyone out. It all fits. First you convince me and Muffie that Ariadne's dead. You must have known the entire time that she was alive. Then you put that disgusting mouse in my sweet roll and now you're pretending that someone put a snake in your suitcase. You don't want to stay here and you know snakes in the house would be the one sure thing to make Mother want to leave."

Before Quentin could respond to Elliot's accusations, a high-pitched wail sounded from the other end of the hall.

"Muffie!" Elliot cried. "What have you done to her?"

"Nothing, potato head." Quentin shoved past his brother and ran into the hall. "I'm going to see if she's okay. You guard the snake."

"I'm not staying in a room with a coral snake, no way." Elliot leapt after his brother into the hall.

"Well, shut the door then, we don't want it to escape!" Quentin shouted over his shoulder.

Meanwhile Muffie was screaming hysterically in her room. As he reached for the doorknob, Quentin braced himself for another snake, or dead mouse, but nothing prepared him for what he and Elliot found.

Muffie's bedspread was covered with insects — dozens of them — centipedes, beetles, silverfish, all squirming and writhing in a dizzying mass. It looked like someone had uprooted a rotten stump after a heavy rain.

"I've never seen so many bugs in my entire life," Quentin breathed in amazement. "There must be over a thousand on the bed."

"They're on the bed, they're in the sheets, they're on my pillow," Muffie shrieked and then she started shuddering. "I feel like they're crawling all over me."

"Where did they come from?" Elliot asked in amazement.

Quentin watched the wriggling mass almost hypnotized by the motion. Suddenly he started singing in time with their rhythm, "The worms crawl in, the worms crawl out, the worms play pinochle on your snout."

Muffie narrowed her eyes at Quentin. "You did

this to me," she hissed, "and I'm telling."

She made a move for the door and nearly stepped on a centipede that had fallen off the bed and was now flipping around on the floor. "Oh, ick!" Muffie cried, leaping out of the way. "I think I'm going to throw up."

"Well, don't barf here," Elliot drawled. "It'll be a major mess." He took a look at his brother, who was still staring in fascination at the bugs, and said, "On second thought, go ahead and puke. We'll make Quentin eat it. That'll teach him to play tricks on us."

That was the last straw for Muffie. She clapped her hand over her mouth and ran for the bathroom.

"Are you satisfied, Quentin?" Elliot demanded. "You made sure I'll never eat another doughnut again, and now you've forced Muffie to blow chunks."

Quentin turned away from the writhing bugs and faced his brother. "Believe me, Elliot," he said, "I had nothing to do with any of this."

Something in the tone of his brother's voice convinced Elliot that he was telling the truth.

"Well, if you didn't do it, and I didn't do it," he reasoned, "who did?"

Their answer came in an explosion of thunder that shook the windows. The sound was unmistakable: an old woman's cackling laughter. Elliot's eyes grew huge as Quentin answered his question in a hoarse whisper.

"Ariadne."

8

"**Q**uentin!" Mrs. Bullock shouted from down-stairs. "Quentin, are you up there?"

Quentin and Elliot were in the bathroom with Muffie. The boys had made a beeline for it the moment they heard Ariadne's voice in the thunder. Now they stood whispering to their sister, who was busy splashing water on her face.

"I tell you, Muffie," Elliot was saying. "It was *her* voice laughing at us outside your window."

"But that's impossible," Muffie said as she patted her face dry with a towel. "My room is on the second floor. Besides," Muffie lowered her voice. "Ariadne left hours ago."

"Maybe she came back and was standing on the roof outside your window," Quentin replied.

"Quentin!" Mrs. Bullock shouted from down-stairs.

"What does she want now?" Elliot muttered.

"Just ignore her," Quentin said. "We've got more important things to deal with."

"*Quentin!* I am calling you!" By now Mrs. Bul-

67

lock was halfway up the stairs. "I know you can hear me."

Quentin gritted his teeth and threw open the bathroom door. "What do you want?" he barked in irritation.

"Don't you use that tone of voice with me, young man," his mother snapped.

Quentin stared at the floor, trying to look properly remorseful. "Sorry."

"I just wanted to tell you that you have a phone call."

"Phone call?" Quentin squinted one eye shut. "From who? I don't know anyone in Bar Harbor."

"It sounds long distance," Mrs. Bullock said. Then she wiggled her eyebrows. "And it's a girl."

"I don't know any girls," Quentin said. "And even if I did, I wouldn't have told them where I was going for the summer."

"Well, maybe they called your friend Edgar and he told them."

"Edgar doesn't know the phone number here, Mother."

"Look." Mrs. Bullock took a deep breath and her nostrils flared with impatience. "I don't want to argue about it. Just answer the phone. You can ask her yourself how she got your phone number."

Quentin stuck his head back in the bathroom. "I've got a phone call."

"That's weird," Elliot said.

Muffie nodded, smoothing her hair back in

place. "Who would call you? You don't have any friends."

Normally Quentin would have met that remark with a scathing crack about Muffie's geeky girl-friends, but the call was too puzzling. Besides, Muffie was right. Except for weird Edgar Hollins, Quentin really didn't have any friends.

"Well, I better go see who it is."

"Wait," Elliot called. "I'll go with you."

"Just a minute." Muffie grabbed Elliot by the arm and held on tight. "You're not leaving me alone up here with those creepy crawlies. I'm coming, too."

The three children hurried down the stairs faster than they needed to, but it was a relief to escape the second floor with its nightmarish bedrooms.

"You'll be lucky if she didn't hang up," Reg Bullock remarked as Quentin and the others passed by the sitting room. Their father was still reading the morning paper. "You took long enough."

Quentin ignored his father's remark and reached for the black receiver. "Hello? This is Quentin."

"Dear little Quentin . . ."

The voice that whispered into the receiver seemed to carry a chill that stung his ear. Quentin jerked the phone away from his ear, then carefully brought it back so he could speak. "Who — who is this?" he demanded.

"You know who I am," the voice breathed. It sounded very far away.

Quentin's eyes bulged behind his glasses and he quickly covered the receiver with his hand. "It's *her*," he hissed to Muffie and Elliot.

"Ariadne?" Elliot's own eyes now matched Quentin's. "Are you sure?"

Quentin swallowed hard. "Is this Ariadne Belljar?"

"Surprised?"

"Well, yes, a little. You see we thought you were, uh, well . . ."

"Disappointed that I'm not?"

"No, of course not. We were just playing a harmless joke."

"No joke is harmless," Ariadne interrupted. "But I'll forget all that. I've got my children back, and that's all that matters."

"What do you mean?"

A high-pitched laugh cackled so loudly from the receiver that Elliot and Muffie could hear it from where they were standing a few feet away.

"Now that I've got you," Ariadne continued, "I'll never let you go."

"Look, Miss Belljar," Quentin said angrily, "we're sorry we scared you but you don't have to threaten — "

"*Never.*"

"But — "

A dial tone buzzed dully in Quentin's ear. He slammed down the phone. "What a weirdo!"

"Was it really Ariadne?" Elliot asked.

"Yeah, that was her haggy voice, all right."

"Well, at least we know she's alive," Muffie whispered, keeping her voice low so Mr. Bullock wouldn't overhear them.

"She's alive," Quentin muttered under his breath, "and she's nuttier than a fruitcake."

"What do you mean?" Elliot demanded.

"She said something like I've got my children back and now I'll never let you go. Never."

"That's definitely a threat of some kind," Muffie said nervously chewing on her lower lip.

"I'll bet she's the one who put those surprises in our rooms," Elliot whispered.

"But how could she have done it?" Quentin asked. "That would mean she sneaked back this morning while we were downstairs."

"Either that," Elliot whispered, "or she never left."

"You mean, when she woke up from her trance, she hid in the house?" Muffie shivered. "That gives me the creeps."

"But she had to have left the house this morning," Elliot declared. "Otherwise, how could she have called?"

Quentin moved to the front door and turned the dead bolt. "We'll just make sure she doesn't return." As the lock clicked into place, Quentin thought he heard that faint cackling laugh once again. He spun around and faced his brother and sister. "Did you hear that?"

"What?" Muffie asked.

"That laugh."

Elliot shook his head. "It must have been the rain hitting the roof, or something. You're just jumpy."

"All right, children!" Mr. Bullock called from the living room door. His booming voice startled them so much that all three yelped in alarm.

"I guess we're all a little jumpy," Elliot said quietly.

"Listen up," their father announced. "Your mother and I are going to take you into Bar Harbor for a tour of the town."

Muffie wrinkled her nose into her pig face. "Now? It's pouring rain."

Mr. Bullock shrugged. "It always rains in Maine."

"Gee, that would make it my choice for a vacation spot," Quentin said with a phony smile.

"No wisecracks, young man," Mr. Bullock growled. "Now I want all of you to march upstairs, put on your rain gear, and get in the car."

"Upstairs?" Muffie looked at Elliot and Quentin in dismay. "Do I have to?"

Mr. Bullock blew his cheeks out in frustration. "Why do we have to play twenty questions whenever I want to do something?" He grabbed his daughter and pulled her up the stairs. "If you won't get your coat voluntarily, I'll make you get it." Then he shouted over his shoulder, "Elliot! Quentin! Get your coats and get them *now!*"

Muffie had no intention of ever going back into that room with its bed full of creepy-crawly insects. She struggled to get out of her father's grasp but his fingers were locked around her arm in a tight grip. "Ow, you're hurting me."

"If you would act like a normal nine-year-old and cooperate, I wouldn't have to," Mr. Bullock grumbled as he pushed open her bedroom door with his foot.

"Don't make me go in there," Muffie cried. "Those awful bugs . . ."

Her sentence trailed off into nothing. Muffie turned and gasped to Quentin and Elliot, who were standing in the hall outside, waiting to hear their father's reaction. "They're gone!"

"Gone?" Quentin repeated. "All of them?"

"What are gone?" Mr. Bullock demanded as he marched to the oak wardrobe and pulled Muffie's raincoat off its hanger.

"There were thousands of bugs," Muffie said. She circled the room cautiously, peeking under the dressing table and bed, and pulling back the curtain by the window. "Everywhere."

"Well, any old house is going to have a few spiders and moths," Mr. Bullock said as he handed her the red slicker. "But they soon get the hint and leave."

"No, Father, you don't understand," Quentin said. "There were hundreds of insects, *thousands* of them, everywhere."

"Now listen here," Mr. Bullock said sternly. "I

take a lot of lip from you children. But I will not be lied to."

"They're not lying. Come to my room, I'll show you." Elliot grabbed his father's arm. "There was a dead mouse in my jelly doughnut."

"This is ridiculous," Mr. Bullock protested as his children led him to the next room. But when Elliot threw open the door, not only was there no dead mouse but even the doughnuts were gone.

Elliot stood in the doorway, shaking his head. "It was brown and furry, and had a long tail, and its guts were gushing out the side of the doughnut."

"Now, Elliot, that's enough," Mr. Bullock said, looking nervously at Muffie. "Do you want your sister to upchuck?"

"She already did," Elliot replied. "When she saw the bugs."

"Look," Mr. Bullock said, putting his hands on his hips. "I know you didn't want to come to Maine, but all of these repulsive stories are not going to make us leave. So just drop it, all right?"

Muffie and Elliot followed their father back down the stairs in stunned silence. Quentin had rushed ahead of the others to his room, somehow knowing he would find no sign of the snake. He was right. The room was completely empty. He got his windbreaker and came back into the hall.

"I don't get it," he muttered to himself. "I just don't get it."

A soft scratching at the window caught his attention and he lifted his head to see what was making the noise. What Quentin saw almost made him faint dead away.

Pressed against the glass was the unforgettable face of Ariadne Belljar. Her lips were parted in a grotesque smile. The face seemed to be floating, almost as if there were no body attached to her head.

"Aaaaaaaahhhhhhhhhhhh!"

Quentin dropped his coat and flew down the steps. His mother and father were just about to go out the front door when he zoomed past them out onto the porch.

"I saw her," he hissed to Muffie and Elliot, who were waiting on the stoop. "At the window." Without a moment's hesitation they took to their heels toward the safety of the van.

"Lock the doors, quick," Quentin instructed the others. Then he rolled down the window and shouted to his parents, "Come on, let's get going."

"Look, Reg," Mrs. Bullock said, pointing to the waiting children in the van.

"I know." He smiled, a real happy grin for the first time since the start of the vacation. "I think there's hope for this family yet."

As they drove down the drive, Muffie glanced nervously behind her and caught her breath.

"Oh, no!"

Elliot and Quentin turned at the same time and gasped. A dark figure was standing motionless among the trees outside the house.

9

"We can have her arrested for breaking and entering, harassment, and vandalism," Quentin whispered as the van rolled along the winding road to Bar Harbor. "Just ask Father."

"We can't ask him," Elliot said, feeling under the car seat for a Reese's peanut butter cup that he had stashed away the day before. "Then we'd have to tell him about Ariadne showing up and our trying to scare her."

"You're right." Quentin leaned back in his seat with a sigh. "Then we'd be sent away to military school for sure."

"So how are we going to get her to leave us alone?" Muffie asked, pulling her skirt away from Elliot's side of the seat to make sure he didn't smear any chocolate on her. He already had a fleck of chocolate on his chin and a chunk of peanut butter in his lap. The wrapper lay where he'd carelessly tossed it on the floor.

"I say we talk to her boss," Quentin said. "They'll tell her to shape up or she's fired. And let's face it, where is an old, ugly hag like her going to find another job?"

"That's a great idea," Elliot said as he systematically licked the chocolate off each pudgy finger. "But we don't know the address for this Eternally Yours Sitter Service."

"Yes, we do." Quentin pulled a yellowing piece of paper out of his shirt pocket. "I took this after Father made the phone call last night."

By this time the van had turned onto the street leading into the center of old Bar Harbor. They instantly joined a parade of cars slowly making their way into the tiny village. The rain had finally stopped. Now the sun was starting to peek out from behind the clouds.

"Great. Wonderful." Reg Bullock sighed as he leaned his elbow on the armrest of his seat. "I drive eight hours to get away from the rat race of New York City, only to end up stuck in a full-fledged traffic jam in Maine."

"Reg?" Mrs. Bullock patted his knee. "Why don't we just park the car and walk into town?"

"Park!" He threw up his hands. "Where? There isn't a spot in sight."

"There was a parking spot about two blocks back," Elliot informed his father.

Mr. Bullock shot him a sour smile through the rearview mirror. "Oh, that's really helpful, Elliot. Why didn't you speak up when you saw it?"

"Because I thought you'd seen it, and deliberately didn't choose it."

Mr. Bullock scowled but said nothing. His son was right. He *had* seen the parking space but if there was one thing Reginald Bullock III hated, it was walking when he didn't have to.

They cruised slowly by a restaurant with striped awnings bordering several art galleries on their right. On their left was the village square filled with hikers with backpacks, tourists with cameras and picnic baskets, and elderly couples wearing matching golf shirts, shorts, and visors.

Muffie stared idly at the crowd on the green, amazed at how many people looked awful in shorts. Especially the old ones with their brown, wrinkled knees and sagging thighs. Thinking of old people and drooping flesh made her think of Ariadne, and she shivered.

Quentin was looking out the window, too, but not at the tourists. He held the address of the sitter service clutched tightly in his hand as he watched for street signs. "Thirty-one and a half Cottage Street," he murmured out loud.

"Cottage Street?" Elliot leaned forward between his parents' seats. "There it is, Quentin."

"Stop the car!"

Quentin yelled so loudly that Mr. Bullock slammed on the brakes. Elliot, who was already wedged between the two front seats, plunged the rest of the way forward into the dashboard.

"My nose!" he cried. "I think it's broken."

"What's the idea scaring me like that?" Mr. Bullock bellowed.

"I'm sorry, Father," Quentin said, trying to sound as polite and respectful as possible. "But we need to get out here."

"What, have you got an appointment?" Mrs. Bullock asked sarcastically.

Muffie crossed her fingers behind her back. "Sort of. But it's very important that we get out of the car."

Since the van was stopped, Quentin took the opportunity to slide open the door. "We'll be back in an hour."

"Back where?" his father asked. "We're in traffic, for God's sake."

"Uh . . ." Quentin looked around quickly and spotted a tiny ice cream shop. "Over there. The Yankee Dipper. We'll meet you there."

Before either parent could respond, Quentin, Elliot, and Muffie had hopped out of the van, and slammed the door. As they hurried down the sidewalk, they could hear their father beating the steering wheel and shouting, "I swear those can't be my children. They just can't be."

The children made their way down Cottage Street, making sure to step around the big puddles of water.

The street was lined with salt water taffy and chocolate shops, ice cream parlors, little pastry shops that sold all kinds of blueberry tarts and muffins, and little stands selling corn dogs and popcorn. Elliot wanted to stop at them all, but Quentin refused to stop.

"Come *on*," Elliot pleaded. "I'm starved."

"Stop thinking about your stomach, and start thinking about Ariadne," Muffie replied.

"Who may at this moment be hunting down more furry creatures to stuff in a corn dog or a muffin," Quentin reminded his brother.

Elliot felt his stomach do a flip-flop as he thought of that ghastly mouse exploding out of a corn dog with its mouth open and its little tongue sticking out to the side. He promptly lost his appetite.

"This street seems too fancy to have a baby-sitting service on it," Muffie said, looking up at the carved wooden signs hanging outside the antique and curio shops.

"Eternally Yours was in business forty years ago," Quentin remarked, "long before this town heard of fancy shops or the word "tourist." Look for the place that seems the oldest."

"Here's number thirty-one." Elliot pointed to a carved black-and-white bird with a bright orange beak and odd little webbed feet. "Puffin Rock. It's a souvenir shop."

"Thirty-one and a *half* is the address, dimwit," Quentin said, continuing on by the store. He passed an alley and stopped at the next shop. It was a bicycle rental shop called SpokeSong. A bright red thirty-three was painted above the door. He backed up to the alley again and shrugged. "It's got to be down there."

Muffie took one look at the narrow passageway choked with mud puddles and piles of trash, and crossed her arms. "I'm not going down there," she declared. "It's filthy and I might get my dress dirty."

Elliot, who still had some chocolate on his hands, reached over and smeared a brown streak across the front of her dress. "There. Now you don't have to worry about getting your dress mussed up. It's already dirty."

Muffie looked down at the stain in horror. "I'm telling," she finally managed to gasp.

"Go ahead," Elliot said, nonchalantly. "I'm not worried."

"That's good," Quentin called. "Because we've got much bigger problems to worry about."

Quentin was standing in front of a torn screen door at the end of the alley. When Muffie and Elliot joined him, he pointed to the door behind the screen. Painted on the transom glass in chipped gold paint were some letters, which Muffie read out loud.

" 'Ally You'? What's that supposed to mean?"

Quentin threw open the screen door to get a closer look at the glass. "Look, birdbrain, some of the letters have chipped away but I'm certain it once said 'Eternally Yours.' "

"Once?" Elliot repeated. "Does that mean it's closed?"

Quentin cupped his hands around the side of his face and peered inside. "The place is a wreck. It looks like no one's been here for years."

Elliot tried the doorknob and, to his surprise,

it was unlocked. "Look," he whispered. "It's open."

"I'm not going in there," Muffie said. "And it's not because I'm afraid I'll get dirty, either. It's because it's against the law."

"Well, we sure won't get arrested for stealing," Quentin joked as he stepped over a wooden chair that lay on its side. "There's absolutely nothing to take."

Muffie reluctantly followed the boys into the ramshackle office.

A photograph of President Eisenhower hung crookedly on one wall over a set of empty bookshelves. In the far corner was a gray metal desk with a broken swivel chair behind it. Behind the desk was a bulletin board. A list of typed names was thumbtacked to it, along with several faded newspaper clippings curling with age.

Muffie stood just inside the door, looking around the room with distaste. Quentin was poking into everything. He pulled one of the file cabinet drawers open and, instead of manila folders, he found an old chipped coffee cup. "Looks like they shut down from lack of business," he commented.

Elliot investigated the desk and discovered a half-eaten roll of Lifesavers in the center drawer. He peeled back the wrapping and gingerly removed the top wintergreen Lifesaver, then popped the second one in his mouth. It was a little squishy but otherwise not bad at all. He smiled and turned to his brother. "If Eternally Yours shut down, then how did Father call Ariadne?"

Muffie was shuffling through a pile of old newspapers spread out on the floor and her foot kicked against something hard. She pulled up a black phone by its cord and said, "Here's the telephone."

"Check the number," Quentin said, examining the note he'd brought with him. "Beechwood-5789."

"That's it," Muffie said. As she handed the phone to Quentin, the split wire came with it. "Wait a minute. It's not connected."

"No, the cord's been cut." Quentin peered at the frayed ends of the connecting wires and plastic casing, which was badly cracked. "A long time ago, too."

"That is weird," Muffie said, scurrying away from the phone as if the object itself held some evil power.

"You want to talk weird," Elliot said, popping the last of the wintergreen Lifesavers in his mouth, "listen to this." He read out loud from one of the clippings tacked to the bulletin board. "Woman reported missing by sitter service. July 14, 1953."

Quentin dumped the disconnected phone on the desk and hurried to Elliot's side. They read the rest of the report in unison.

"The Eternally Yours Sitter Service reported to Bar Harbor police today that one of their employees, a Miss Ariadne Belljar, has been missing since Friday afternoon. The owner of the service,

83

Mrs. Fred Lucerne, told Detective Harvey Moon that Miss Belljar had gone to work for the Kensington family in June." Elliot looked over his shoulder and said, "Isn't that the name in the nursery?"

"Yes!" Quentin gasped. "Keep reading."

"After four weeks, Miss Belljar suddenly disappeared. She doesn't answer her phone, and she hasn't picked up her paycheck, Mrs. Lucerne told this reporter. If Miss Belljar were sick, she certainly would have called. She is our most efficient sitter. The Kensingtons could not be reached for comment."

"Maybe they went on vacation and took Ariadne with them," Muffie said.

Quentin shook his head. "It says in this clipping that she is required to report to the sitter service about those things."

"Wow!" Elliot gasped. "Ariadne is a missing person."

"Not any more," Muffie said. "We found her. Maybe there's some sort of reward."

"Maybe she's not just a missing person," Quentin mused, "but a fugitive from the law. That would explain her weird behavior."

"Read this other clipping," Elliot urged. "You may be right."

Quentin leaned in and read over his brother's shoulder:

"District court Judge Bradford Chase Kensington, his wife, and two children have been reported missing. Police Chief Delbert 'Bud' Bickle believes there may be some link between the Kensingtons' abrupt disappearance and that of Miss Ariadne Belljar, formerly of the Eternally Yours Sitter Service and, until she vanished, an employee of the Kensington family. Foul play is suspected."

"Foul Play," Muffie repeated. By now she had joined her brothers at the bulletin board. "You mean, like murder?"

Quentin took his glasses off and polished them carefully on his shirt. "Maybe Ariadne murdered the entire Kensington family, ran away, and now almost forty years later, she's come back." He put his glasses back on his nose. "They say criminals always return to the scene of the crime."

Elliot swallowed the last of his Lifesaver in a big gulp. "That would mean that we have a murderer after us."

"But why does she want to get us?" Muffie asked. When her two brothers raised their eyebrows at her, she said, "Okay, okay, I know we weren't exactly nice to her but that's no reason to want to kill us."

Quentin snapped his fingers. "Maybe she thinks we're them."

"Them who?" Elliot asked.

"The Kensingtons. Of course!" Quentin paced restlessly around the room, rustling his feet through the newspapers like leaves on an autumn day. "That would explain Ariadne's weird words to me on the phone. She said, 'I've got my children back.' "

"You mean, she killed the people who used to live here but maybe she forgot that she killed them, and now she thinks they're back?" Muffie asked.

"Exactly."

"She'd have to be crazy to think up something like that," Elliot said.

"Of course she's crazy," Muffie said. "Who else but a crazy person would fake being dead and then fill our rooms with gross creepie crawlers and then climb on the roof just so she could make faces at us through our windows?"

"Muffie's right," Quentin said. "I'd say the woman is certifiable."

Elliot flopped against the wall. "This is just great. We have a homicidal maniac after us, and no one to turn to for help."

"Why don't we tell Mother and Father?" Muffie said. "Father will have her put in jail."

"Yeah, right." Quentin rolled his eyes. "We tell them that a sitter showed up last night and, after we gave her a hard time, she decided to fake her own death and then hide in the house so she could terrorize us and finally murder us. Do you really think they'd believe that, coming from us?"

All three children stared at one another and shook their heads. "No way."

"Then there's only one place to go," Quentin said, pulling the clippings off the bulletin board and tucking them in the pocket of his wind-breaker. "The police."

This time Muffie folded her arms across her chest and rolled her eyes. "Oh, yeah, sure. You think the police will believe that story when our parents won't?"

Quentin stared at his sister, completely stone-faced. "Yes."

"But why?"

"Because they don't know us," he explained. "We'll tell them we're Reginald Bullock III's children — *the* Reginald Bullock III. We've just come up from New York. Our parents went to a party and while they were gone, a weird woman appeared and harassed us. I'll hand them these clippings, they'll see that Ariadne must have come back, and — " He shrugged. "They'll place her under arrest and toss her in jail."

"Just like that?" Elliot asked.

"Just like that," Quentin replied breezily. "Now come on."

He hurried out the door into the alley, hoping that his brother and sister didn't see the worry in his eyes. There was one little fact that had been troubling him but he didn't want to mention it and freak them out.

Their father had called the Eternally Yours Sitter Service the night before. All of them had heard the call. But how could the phone have rung if the line at Eternally Yours had been disconnected years ago?

10

"We'd like to report a murderer on the loose," Elliot declared as the three children stepped through the doors of the Bar Harbor police station.

It was a small brick building near the boat docks. A lone patrol car was parked in front and a heavy-set policeman was sitting behind a desk, drinking a cup of coffee while he read a magazine. The officer looked up in surprise at Quentin's announcement. "Who's been murdered?"

"An entire family," Quentin replied.

"Ah." The policeman sat forward in his chair with a grin. "An entire family of what? Lobsters?"

Quentin pursed his lips. He hated it when grown-ups talked down to him. "Is there someone here we can talk to who has the brains to listen?" he demanded. "Like your boss?"

The officer's smile faded. "Don't push it, kid. There's no one else here. I'm the whole department."

"Then you should listen to my brother," Muffie

said, "because he's telling the truth."

The policeman heaved a sigh and grabbed a pad of paper. "Okay, give me the details of this so-called murder."

"Well, I don't have many," Quentin admitted. "But these might explain a few things." He slid the newspaper clippings across the desk.

"Hmm." The officer scratched his bald spot and settled back into his chair to read them.

Muffie and Quentin watched intently to see the officer's reaction. In the meantime, Elliot had spotted a candy machine on the far side of the room. He sauntered over and slipped two quarters into the slot, then pulled the knob for an Almond Joy. He liked Almond Joys because they came in two sections and he always felt like he was getting more for his money.

The policeman looked up from the clippings. "I was here when this happened. I vaguely remember something about it, but what does this have to do with murder?"

Quentin put both hands on the desk and, leaning across it, stuck his face up close to the policeman's. "She's back."

"Who's back?"

"Ariadne Belljar. We're renting Maldemere, the old Kensington place, and Ariadne showed up last night."

"And we figured that since she was a fugitive from the law besides being a missing person," Muffie chimed in, "there might be a large reward."

Quentin dug his elbow into his sister's side. "Forget the reward," he growled. "That's not why we're here."

She rubbed the spot where he'd jabbed her. "Well, if there is a reward, I think we deserve to get it," she pouted. "After all, we found the murderer."

"Wait a minute. Wait a minute." The officer pushed his chair back from the desk and stood up. "First of all, there has been no murder."

"No murder?" Elliot mumbled through a mouthful of chocolate and coconut. "That's ridiculous."

"What about the baby clothes?" Muffie demanded. "And the tea set, and the toys?"

The policeman shot her a baffled look.

"The house we're renting still has the people's clothes in it," Quentin explained, "as if they had just up and vanished."

"That's kind of how it was," the officer said. He rubbed his bald spot again, then scratched behind his ear and a couple of places on his neck. "I was just a kid at the time but lemme see . . . as I recall, there was a big *brouhaha* about the Kensingtons. He was the district judge. Just appointed, too. Only been in town a few months. They bought Maldemere and then they just up and left in the middle of the night."

"Why?"

The officer shrugged. "Something frightened them. So badly that it was several months before the judge let anyone know his whereabouts."

"Did they ever come back?" Muffie asked.

He shook his head. "Not that I know of. The house just sat there, crumbling. That is, until this summer when the judge's kids decided to rent it out. They're all grown up now, you see. He died some years ago, I guess."

"What about Ariadne Belljar?" Quentin asked. "The woman who worked for them?"

"I don't remember anything about her." The policeman squinted one eye shut. "In fact, this is a small town and I've never heard of anyone by that name."

"How about the Eternally Yours Sitter Service?" Elliot asked.

He chuckled. "Oh, yeah, I remember that place. Several old maids set it up, and for a while our parents were really gung ho about it. Then . . ." He shrugged. "They must have closed down. Maybe the ladies died. They were pretty ancient."

"But Ariadne — the missing person in that article." Quentin jabbed the yellowing clipping with his finger. "She has come back. She showed up last night and she was at the house again today. Or at least we think she was."

"Maybe she wanted to see what the place looked like after all those years," the officer suggested.

"No, it's not like that," Muffie insisted. "It's worse. Much worse. She put mice in our doughnuts, snakes in our suitcases, and bugs in our beds — "

"Even though we know for a fact that she hates

that kind of thing," Elliot added. "Especially rodents."

The policeman stared at them for a few moments in silence. Finally he said, "Okay. You kids have had your fun. Now I think it's time for you to move along."

"But — "

"I *mean* it," the officer said sternly. "I don't have time to waste on this garbage."

"Tell him, Quentin," Muffie pleaded. "Make him understand."

Quentin had been silent for some time. "I think the man's right," he said abruptly. "We better leave."

"*What?*" Elliot looked as though he were going to burst with indignation. "But what about harassment, and breaking and entering, and vandalism, and all that other stuff — "

"We'll talk about it later." Quentin grabbed his brother and sister by the arms and ushered them toward the door. "Come on. Mother and Father are waiting for us. Thank you, officer."

They left him leaning against his desk, scratching his head. The minute they were back on the street, Quentin said, "I think we've got a real mystery on our hands."

"I'll say we do," Elliot grumbled as he licked the last few flecks of chocolate stuck to the Almond Joy wrapper. "Here we had the perfect opportunity to turn Ariadne in, and you just blew it off."

"That's because we can't prove anything," Quentin retorted. He led his brother across the street into the park in the village square. "We have to catch her in the act."

"You mean, like, right in the house?" Muffie asked. "I really don't want to go back in there. She's too weird."

"Besides," Elliot added, "maybe she's not there anymore."

"Oh, she'll be there all right," Quentin said.

"How can you be sure?" Muffie asked.

Quentin took a deep breath and faced his siblings. "Because I think she lives there."

"*What?*" Elliot and Muffie yelped so loudly that several people in the park turned to look at them.

"It all fits," Quentin whispered excitedly. "The Kensingtons move to town, buy a house, and hire Ariadne. Suddenly they leave town, scared out of their wits, and the house sits empty for years. But it's not really empty — "

"Ariadne is living there!" Muffie gasped. "You mean she was the one who scared the Kensingtons into leaving so she could have the house?"

"Exactly," Quentin replied. "And now that it's for rent, she wants to scare *us* away from the place."

"And it seems like she'll stop at nothing to make us stay away," Elliot whispered.

"What are we going to do?" Muffie asked.

"Refuse to go back in there," Quentin replied. "Our lives could be at stake."

"Father will just drag us back." Muffie rubbed the sore spot on her arm where Mr. Bullock had grabbed her earlier that day. "You know he will."

"Not if we pull out all the stops," Quentin said with a wicked grin.

"You mean throw a tantrum?" Muffie asked.

Quentin nodded. "Throw a tantrum, get a deadly disease — anything you can think of to keep from going back inside that house. And if worse come to worst, we'll show them these clippings."

A sudden breeze came up and whipped the newspaper clippings out of Quentin's hand. The children watched in astonishment as the wind lifted the clippings into the air.

As they watched the pieces of paper flutter out of sight, Elliot murmured, "I don't like that woman. I don't like that house. And I really don't like this weather."

"There you are!" their mother's voice called from across the park. "Where have you three been? We were supposed to meet at the Yankee Dipper, remember?"

"Sorry, Mother," Elliot said as he watched her hurry to join them. "But we got sidetracked."

"Well, your father is storming all over town looking for you," Mrs. Bullock scolded mildly. She was eating a soft ice cream cone and wiped some drips off her fingers with a paper napkin. "When he gets back here, don't push him. He's had a terrible afternoon."

"What happened?" Quentin asked.

"The real estate agency said we arrived too early," her mother explained. "That's why the place was such a mess."

"Does that mean we're going to leave?" Muffie asked hopefully.

"Certainly not. But we're not paying the rent until that place is cleaned up." Mrs. Bullock shooed them ahead of her with her arms. "Come along now, we're running late as it is."

"I think we should leave," Elliot declared. "They'll never get it clean. It's been sitting boarded up for forty years. That's a lot of dirt."

"Well, it's about time!" a voice bellowed from across the tiny park. The children looked up to see their father marching toward them, his arms swinging stiffly by his sides. "I want you in the van by the time I count three. One — "

"Reg," Mrs. Bullock interrupted in a soothing voice, "the children don't even know where the van is."

"They've got eyes, don't they?" he snapped. "All they have to do is — "

Suddenly Quentin dropped to the ground and his anguished groan drowned out the rest of his father's sentence. Quentin folded his arms to his chest, rolled his eyes back in his head, and jerked his body in short convulsions.

"Oh, my God," Mr. Bullock cried in alarm. "What's the matter with Quentin?"

"Nothing." Mrs. Bullock took another lick of her

ice cream cone and dabbed her lips with her napkin. "He's faking an epileptic seizure." She knelt down by her writhing son and said, "You pulled that *last* summer vacation, remember?"

Quentin stopped his pathetic groaning and opened his eyes. He had forgotten all about that episode. He thought he'd only used the seizure ruse at boarding school. Now he felt silly. "Just joking."

When Elliot saw that Quentin's trick hadn't worked, he decided to try his own illness. Clutching his right side, he bellowed, "Ow, it hurts. My side hurts."

Mrs. Bullock watched her chubby son hop around in a circle, holding his side. "What is it, Elliot, appendicitis?"

Elliot nodded his head. "Yes, I'm sure it is."

"Then it should be hurting on the other side, my little genius." Mrs. Bullock dropped the remains of her ice cream cone in a trash can.

"Mother!" Muffie shouted suddenly. "Oh, Mother."

"Now what's wrong with you?" Mr. Bullock demanded.

"Nothing's wrong with me," Muffie replied. "But I think there may be something wrong with our house."

"It's filthy, I know," Mrs. Bullock replied. "But I told you the rental agency is going to take care of that."

"Not our rental house, our *real* house in New

York. I think that I left, um, I left . . ." Muffie looked at her brothers for help. Quentin was lying motionless on the ground, too humiliated to get up. Elliot was tenderly probing his stomach on the right, then the left. Muffie gave up on them and blurted, "I think I left the stove on, and the faucet was still running in the bathroom when we left."

"You *think* you did this?" Mr. Bullock exclaimed. "Or you did it."

Quentin sprang to his feet, seizing this new opportunity. "She did it. I watched her turn the faucet on. Water was spraying everywhere."

Mr. Bullock's face turned a bright red as a vein in his forehead throbbed angrily. "Are you telling me that you watched your sister deliberately flood our home?"

"Now, Reg, calm down," Mrs. Bullock cut in. "You used the bathroom last, remember? Was the water running?"

Mr. Bullock's flushed face abruptly returned to normal. "No, it wasn't. And the burners weren't on, either. I checked them. And I did all this while you children were fighting in the hallway."

Muffie tried one last attempt. "Are you absolutely sure?"

"*Yes, I'm sure!*" Mr. Bullock roared. "And why are you lying to me?"

He didn't give his daughter time to answer. Instead Mr. Bullock marched across the park toward the Yankee Dipper. The van was parked in front of the ice cream parlor. He climbed in the driver's side and, rolling down his window, called, "I'm counting *one*, I'm counting — "

"We better get in the van," Elliot moaned. "He's got that you're-going-to-military-school-for-the-rest-of-your-life sound."

"*Two!*"

Muffie held back. "I'll get in the van. But you can't force me into that house. Not if that witch is still living there."

"*Two and a half — *"

"All right, we're coming!" Quentin cried. He grabbed his sister by the hand and pulled her across the street toward the van. "You won't have to go in there, Muffie," he whispered under his breath. "I'm going to talk to Father."

"What are you going to tell him?" Elliot was huffing to keep up with them.

"The truth," his brother muttered. "The whole truth, and nothing but the truth."

"*Three!*"

Reg Bullock slammed the van in gear and the children barely had time to hop in before he floored the gas pedal, leaving a trail of rubber on the street.

As they sped home, Elliot said nervously, "I hope you know what you're doing, Quentin."

"It'll all work out," Quentin said, biting his lip in apprehension. "Just trust me."

11

But Quentin didn't tell his parents the truth. Not exactly. He left out some important parts — such as the fact that they thought they had frightened Ariadne Belljar to death. In fact, he left out most of the evening's events, condensing the story to the following exchange.

"Father, after you and Mother left for the Randolphs, a really weird woman showed up saying she was from the Eternally Yours Sitter Service."

"What?" Mr. Bullock nearly swerved off the road. Luckily they had already left the town and were winding their way up the cliff to Maldemere, so there were no other cars on the road.

"We didn't tell you because she left right away," Quentin explained hurriedly, "and we were afraid you'd think we chased her off."

Mr. Bullock met his son's eye in the rearview mirror. "Really?"

"I wouldn't have mentioned it," Quentin continued, "except that she came back today. I saw her face at the window. And she called me on the telephone." Quentin tapped Mrs. Bullock on the shoulder. "You heard her voice, Mother."

She nodded. "I think he's telling us the truth, Reg."

"So what does this woman want?" Mr. Bullock asked as they turned into the driveway of Maldemere.

"I'm not sure," Quentin admitted. "But, Father, I have reason to believe that she's hiding inside the house."

Mr. Bullock braked the van to a halt in front of the house. "Now that's a lot of nonsense."

"Listen to him, Daddy," Muffie pleaded. "We all think she's in there."

"Impossible." Mr. Bullock held up his key ring. "I locked the front door. How could she have gotten in?"

Elliot spoke for the first time on the ride home. "Maybe she has a key, too."

"Daddy?" Muffie put her hand on her father's arm and, using her best little girl voice, said *"Please* don't make us go in there. We're scared."

Mr. Bullock turned in his seat and studied his children's faces. "You kids really are spooked, aren't you?"

All three nodded emphatically.

A smile spread slowly across his face. He gave his wife a wink and declared, "Well, I'll go in first and make sure this scary old bogeywoman isn't there." Then he hopped out of the van and swaggered up to the front door.

"Oh, great," Quentin groaned. "He thinks this is his big chance to show us what a brave daddy he is."

"Now don't speak disrespectfully of your father," Mrs. Bullock chided. "You know as well as I do that there's no one in the house so let's just put an end to this nonsense." She got out and followed her husband up the paved walk.

"I'm not staying out here by myself," Muffie muttered, sliding open the door and scrambling onto the gravel. "She could be hiding in the trees again."

Elliot grimaced. "No kidding."

The boys jumped out and the three of them clutched hands as they made their way gingerly to the front porch. Mr. Bullock had just unlocked the door and was making a big show of shouting, "Hello! Anybody home?"

Mrs. Bullock put her hand on her husband's shoulder. "Oh, look, Reg, the kids are actually holding hands," she said in a loud whisper. "I knew this trip to Maine would be good for them."

The children instantly dropped their hands to their sides. The last thing they needed was for their parents to think they were having *fun*.

"No scary woman in the foyer," their father announced loudly from just inside the door. Quentin looked at his siblings and stuck his finger down his throat. There was no option left but to follow their parents into the house.

Just as he stepped over the threshold, Elliot

thought he saw something move in the bushes by the corner of the house. But when he turned to look, there was nothing there.

"I'll just take this *gun* from the front closet," Mr. Bullock boomed as he pulled out an umbrella. "Now anyone who might be in here ought to think twice before he duels with the Bullocks."

Mrs. Bullock covered her mouth with her hand to stifle her giggles. "Oh, Reg!"

Quentin rolled his eyes and whispered, "He sounds like a character from a bad Western."

Thrusting the umbrella in front of him like a fencing sword, Mr. Bullock charged into the library. "Haiiee-*yah!*" Mrs. Bullock clutched her stomach and collapsed on the stairs, gasping with laughter.

While their parents joked around, Quentin, Elliot, and Muffie searched the ground floor in earnest, looking for little signs that might betray Ariadne's presence.

"Was the kitchen door closed when we left?" Muffie whispered. " 'Cause it's closed now."

"I don't remember," Elliot said. "Should we peek inside?"

Quentin shook his head. "I don't think Ariadne is down here. I bet she's upstairs somewhere."

By now Mr. Bullock had returned to the foyer and was tickling Mrs. Bullock with the umbrella. As they watched her squeal with laughter, the children realized they had never seen their parents acting so goofily. They looked like they were really having fun, which was particularly strange since the children knew all their lives might be in danger.

"Now let's check out the demons on the second floor," Mr. Bullock declared. He charged up the stairs, taking the steps two at a time.

"Wait for me, Reg," Mrs. Bullock cried. "I wouldn't miss this for the world."

"Father, be careful," Elliot called but the parents had already disappeared into Muffie's room.

Suddenly the wind outside picked up and a shutter slammed loudly against the side of the house. Muffie let out a shriek and for the second time that day grabbed Quentin and Elliot by the hand. The boys didn't jerk their hands away. The three of them stood motionless in the foyer, listening for Ariadne. But nothing happened.

The crash of the shutter interrupted their parents' horseplay. The children heard their mother gasp, "Oh, look at the time. Reg, if we don't hurry, we'll be late for the Randolphs." She ran out of Muffie's room and hurried down the hall toward the master bedroom. "We've got just enough time to comb our hair, change our clothes, and go."

"Go?" Muffie skipped up the stairs to her parents' room. "Where are we going?"

"You're not going anywhere," Mrs. Bullock said, as she threw open the doors to her wardrobe. "Your father and I are going to the Randolphs."

"But you were just there last night," Muffie protested as her mother pulled a white linen skirt and a blouse with a blue sailor collar off their hangers.

"They've invited us for tea and croquet." Mrs. Bullock hopped across the room toward her vanity, removing her tan espadrilles and switching to low navy blue pumps.

Muffie looked out the window at the darkening sky. "In this weather? You'll get rained out."

"If we do, we'll just come home," her mother replied as she slipped into the skirt and pulled the blouse over her head.

"But why can't we come, too?" Muffie asked, following her mother down the hall into the bathroom.

"Because it's for adults." Mrs. Bullock stood looking in the mirror above the sink and hurriedly pulled a comb through her hair.

"We won't say a word," Muffie promised. "We'll sit quietly in the corner."

Mrs. Bullock paused with her comb in midair. "Like you did when we were invited to Sydney Crenshaw's for Christmas? It's lucky the tree didn't catch fire when you kids knocked it over. But those glass ornaments were irreplaceable. Syd still won't speak to me."

As her mother shut the medicine cabinet door, Muffie caught a glimpse of a face reflected in the mirror — a face with bloodshot eyes, a hawklike nose, and pointed teeth, standing in the hallway behind her. She gasped and spun to look, but no one was in the hall.

Muffie shut her eyes, trying not to cry from fear. "Don't leave us alone," she whimpered.

"You did just fine last night!" Mrs. Bullock noticed her daughter's trembling lip and said sternly, "Tears aren't going to get you anywhere. Now your father made sure that that nasty woman isn't here so you have nothing to be afraid of." Then she patted her daughter on the head. "It's only for a little while. If it makes you feel any better, I promise we'll be back before dark."

"It doesn't make me feel any better," Muffie whimpered. She was afraid to open her eyes for fear she might see that awful face again. "By then it could be too late."

Meanwhile the boys were working on their father, who was changing his clothes in the guest bedroom.

"Couldn't you just drop us downtown?" Quentin pleaded. "We'll look around, do a little shopping, and then you can pick us up on the way home from the Randolphs."

"The Randolphs live in the opposite direction," Mr. Bullock said, tucking his pale yellow polo shirt into his chinos.

"Then we'll take a cab home," Elliot suggested from his perch on the edge of the bed.

"That's ridiculous." Mr. Bullock opened the wardrobe to pull out his navy blue blazer. "You children stay here. I'm sure you can find something to occupy your time."

Just as his father was shutting the door, Quentin caught sight of a pair of legs hanging at eye level inside the closet. They were encased in dark hose and black lace-up shoes, and swung slightly from side to side.

"Father!" he yelped. "Look out!"

"Huh?" Mr. Bullock sprang backwards. "What's the matter?"

Quentin could only point soundlessly at the closet.

Mr. Bullock re-opened the closet. It was empty. No legs, no lace-up shoes. Just his shirts and jackets hanging in a neat row.

"Just what are you trying to pull, young man?" he snapped.

"But it was Ariadne," Quentin gasped.

"I am not listening to another word about that woman from either of you," his father interrupted. "Do I make myself clear?"

Quentin didn't answer. And Elliot *couldn't* answer. He sat mesmerized as an immense hairy rat dragged a dismembered hand past the open doorway down the hall. The hand was green from decay, with bloated fingers and long yellow nails. Elliot's jaw flapped open and shut like a fish.

"*Do I make myself clear?*" Mr. Bullock bellowed directly into Elliot's face.

"Ye-yes, sir," Elliot squeaked.

Quentin saw the horrified look on his brother's face and turned to see what had frightened him. All he saw was the worn wooden floor of the corridor.

Mr. Bullock checked his watch and stuck his head into the hall. "Jenny? I'll be in the car."

"I'm right behind you, darling," Mrs. Bullock said as she emerged from her bedroom.

The Bullocks hurried down the main stairs and out the front door without even a good-bye or a backward glance. The children gathered glumly at the upstairs window to watch their parents drive away. As the van disappeared down the drive, a cloud crossed the sun and the temperature in the house seemed to drop ten degrees.

"Did you feel that?" Quentin whispered.

Elliot nodded. "She's here."

Muffie dabbed her eyes, which were brimming with tears. "I've already seen her disgusting face," she murmured. "In the bathroom mirror."

"I saw her feet," Quentin added. "Hanging in the closet."

Elliot glanced nervously over his shoulder at the hall. "I think I saw her hand being dragged past the door by a rat."

Muffie grabbed her brother's arm. "We've got to get away from here."

Quentin shook his head. "She's trying to frighten us but it's got to be an illusion of some sort. All of it."

"You mean, like a magic act?" Elliot asked.

"Exactly. She probably used this stuff on the Kensingtons when they bought the place. And now she's using it on us."

"But where could she be hiding?" Muffie whispered.

Creak-creak. Creak-creak.

"What was that?" Elliot said in a hoarse whisper.

Quentin raised his eyes to the ceiling. "Ariadne. It's got to be." He looked at his brother and sister and narrowed his eyes. "She's in the attic."

12

"**I** don't like this," Muffie moaned. "I don't like it one bit. Why can't we wait until Mother and Daddy come home, and *they* can deal with her?"

"Because Ariadne won't let them see her," Quentin said as he led them into the kitchen. "She's trying to torment us." He rummaged through every drawer and shelf, gathering knives, cast-iron frying pans, and anything else that could be used as a weapon.

"What are we supposed to do with these?" Elliot asked as Quentin handed him a paring knife and a shish kebab skewer. "Stab the old bag?"

"If it comes to that." Quentin handed his sister a wooden spatula and a can opener.

"See here, I think she's witchy and ugly and weird," Elliot said, putting his weapons back on the kitchen counter. "But I'm not about to kill anybody."

"I'm not asking you to kill her," Quentin said as he stuffed a set of chopsticks in each of his pockets and picked up a corkscrew. "I just think we would be a bunch of no-brainers if we marched up to the attic unarmed."

"I never agreed to go up into the attic," Muffie cried. "That was your idea. And what's more, since you thought of it, I think you should do it."

Quentin folded his arms and stared at his sister. "Are you forgetting about the face in the mirror, and the thousands of creepy-crawly bugs in your bed?"

"Don't mention those things," Muffie said with a shudder.

"Well, I'm sure Miss Belljar has a lot more tricks up her sleeve if we don't get rid of her now."

"How do you plan on doing that, Mr. Genius?" Elliot asked, picking up a maple bar that was lying with the leftover sweet rolls on the counter. He checked the insides with a poke of his thumb, then stuffed the entire pastry in his mouth.

"I think telling her that we know where she's hiding, and that we're not afraid of her little tricks will probably do it." Quentin wrinkled his nose in disgust at his brother, whose mouth was so full he couldn't close it all the way to chew. "God, Elliot. You are such a gross pig."

Elliot took his forefinger and jabbed the maple bar until he could finally shut his mouth. Then he managed to mumble, "Takes one to know one." As he spoke he reached for the paper plate that held the last two rolls. Just before his hand touched it, the plate slipped sideways and fell to the floor.

"D-d-did you see that?" Elliot stammered. "The thing moved all by itself."

"Yeah, sure it did," Quentin said without looking at his brother. He was busy peering into a small broom closet for possible implements of destruction.

"I'm not kidding." Elliot turned to Muffie. "You saw it, didn't you?"

"I saw the plate hit the floor," Muffie replied. "In your pigginess, you probably knocked it over."

"Have it your way," Elliot yelled. "Don't believe me. But there's no way I'm sticking around here." Elliot spun on his heel and bolted for the kitchen door. Just as his hand hit the swinging door, all the lights went out. The children stood in the darkened kitchen and listened to the fading whine of the refrigerator motor as it wound down. Then everything was quiet.

"Do you think that had anything to do with the storm this morning?" Muffie asked in a tiny voice.

"No." Quentin gestured to the window, which revealed a rectangle of blue afternoon sky outside. "I think it was something — or somebody else — who did that."

"But why would she turn off the electricity?" Elliot demanded. "It's still light outside."

"But it's not light in the attic, I bet you." Quentin pulled open the cabinet doors beneath the sink and peered into the darkness. "We need a candle, or a flashlight."

"I can't believe you're still planning to go through with this," Muffie exclaimed.

"If we don't, we'll spend the next four weeks being terrorized by a decrepit old spinster." Quentin pulled each drawer out onto the floor. Finally a couple of white candles and a box of kitchen matches fell out and tumbled onto the tiles. "Now, come on!"

Muffie hung back as Elliot followed Quentin through the living room into the foyer. But as soon as she realized she was about to be left alone, she cried, "Wait for me. I'm coming, too."

Creak-creak. Creak-creak.

"There's that sound again," Quentin said, looking up the stairs to the darkened hallway. The sound was like a beacon calling to him. He began mounting the stairs, his brother and sister clinging close behind him.

Creak-creak. Creak-creak.

With each step the noise grew louder and louder. When they reached the second floor, Elliot whispered, "I'm going to light the candle. Muffie, you be in charge of the matches. Don't drop them."

Muffie took the box and clutched it tightly in her palm. "Don't go too fast for me," she pleaded. "I hate the dark."

They shuffled slowly past the closed bedroom doors, their eyes fixed on the tiny door at the end of the hall. With each step, the hall became darker and darker. The air seemed to grow colder, too.

"I wish I'd brought a sweater," Muffie whispered.

"I wish I'd brought my armor," Elliot muttered as Quentin reached for the attic door. "I hope she doesn't have a gun."

"Gun?" Quentin hesitated with his hand on the knob. It had never occurred to him that she might be armed. He looked down at the chopsticks in his pocket and the corkscrew in his hand and felt a little foolish. "I'm sure she doesn't," he said out loud, hoping he sounded more confident than he felt. "Otherwise she would have used it by now."

Creak-creak. Creak-creak.

The sound above them was almost deafening.

"What *is* that noise?" Elliot hissed.

"I don't know." Quentin turned the knob and the door opened. He held out his candle and squinted up the dimly lit corridor. Ten narrow steps led to the attic door. "But we're about to find out."

Muffie grabbed ahold of Elliot's elbow while Elliot tucked his fingers through Quentin's belt. Quentin secretly wished someone else were leading the way.

Creak-creak. Creak-creak.

The sound seemed to echo with each step they took on the stairs.

Creak-creak.

When they reached the top step, the noise abruptly stopped.

"She knows," Quentin whispered. "She knows we're here."

"I want Daddy," Muffie whimpered.

"Get a grip," Elliot hissed over his shoulder.

Quentin held the candle up to the door. It was choked with cobwebs that stretched from the top of the doorjamb to the wooden railing. He swiped at them with one hand and they wrapped around his hand like a sticky cocoon.

"Oh, yuck!"

He scraped the rest of the web off on the railing and, taking a deep breath, reached for the black doorknob. He turned it slowly and then pushed forward. Nothing happened. He tried again. "It's locked."

"Oh. Well, I guess we'll have to try another day," Muffie said brightly. She tugged on Elliot's elbow, which automatically pulled Quentin backwards.

"Elliot, stop pulling," Quentin said.

"I'm not," Elliot protested. "It was Muffie."

Quentin turned to scold his sister when he saw a gleam of metal reflect the candle's beam. An old-fashioned skeleton key was hanging on a nail by the door.

"Voilà," he said, lifting it off the nail. "Here, Elliot, hold the candle while I unlock the door."

"The door is locked from this side?" Elliot said as his brother slipped the heavy iron key into the lock. "That's strange."

"What's so strange about that?" Muffie asked.

"Because if you were hiding in the attic, you would lock it from the other side," Elliot explained.

Quentin listened to his brother and knew he was making sense. But he knew there had to be some other explanation. "Maybe it's a two-way," he suggested as he turned the key in the lock. It clicked open and their hearts revved into high gear.

"Wait! Wait!" Muffie pleaded. "Are we totally sure we want to do this?"

Quentin hesitated for only a second. "There's no turning back now," he declared, pushing the door open into the attic.

Their noses were immediately assaulted by a smell that was a thick mixture of mothballs and dust that had been baked in the heat of the enclosed room for years and years. It was sour and sweet all at the same time, like rotten flowers. The children covered their noses.

Quentin couldn't muster the courage to actually step through the door so he stuck his head into the room.

"Ariadne?" To his dismay his voice cracked when he called her name.

There was no answer. He tried again.

"Miss Belljar?"

"She must not be here." Muffie tugged on Elliot's shirt. "Come on, let's go back down."

"Wait!" Quentin said. His eyes had adjusted to the dim light and he stepped far enough inside to peer around the room. It was a long, narrow space with low beams. A few packing crates were stacked near the door, several of which had collapsed with age. What looked like an antique leather trunk lay under one of the rafters, covered with dust. The floor consisted of wide boards that had been placed across the beams. There were only a few safe places to stand. A step off a board meant that you would probably fall through the ceiling of the room below. The only light in the room came from a tiny window at the far end of the attic. It was the broken one that they'd seen from the car. Silhouetted against the light was a woman's profile.

"There she is."

Elliot stepped into the attic behind Quentin and whispered, "It looks like she's sitting down."

Muffie was clinging to Elliot like she was his second skin. She peeked around the side of his shoulder and gasped, "In a rocking chair."

"Of course. That explains the *creak-creak* sound we've been hearing," Quentin murmured over his shoulder.

"Why doesn't she say anything?" Muffie whispered. "She's just sitting there, staring out that broken window."

"I guess she's pretty ticked off at us," Quentin replied. "I'll try to get her to talk." He swallowed hard, then took a few tentative steps toward the silent figure. "Look, Miss Belljar, first of all, we're sorry about that awful trick we played on you last night. We were just being rotten but we never meant for you to get so upset."

Quentin paused and waited for her to say something. The figure didn't respond. He took a few more steps toward her, holding the candle out in front of him to make sure he stepped on the right boards. "We know you think this is your house and you don't want us here. Well, we've got news for you — we don't want to be here either. So you don't need to convince us to leave."

Elliot could see that Quentin was getting nowhere. He leaned forward and declared, "If it were up to us, we'd be out of here in a flash but our parents are the ones forcing us to stay here."

The silhouetted figure remained still. The silence was really uncomfortable.

Muffie hated to be ignored by anyone. She put her hands on her hips and said, "Look here, for your information, we know all about you and the Kensingtons, and how you scared them, and how they ran away in the middle of the night. Well, you can't do that to us. We'll have you arrested first."

There was still no answer from the old woman.

Suddenly Quentin felt silly for being scared of her. The fact that she was doing nothing to stop them, made him bold enough to march across the attic floor right up to her chair and demand an explanation. Elliot and Muffie followed right behind him.

Ariadne was facing away from him, still staring

out the little window, so they couldn't see her face. But as he drew a little closer Quentin noticed Ariadne was wearing the same clothes she had worn the night before — the long black skirt, pointed black shoes, and black blouse. A gray shawl lay draped over her shoulders. Her gray hair was pinned back in a tight bun at the base of her neck as she sat staring out the window.

"Ariadne Belljar!" he shouted angrily. "I'm talking to you."

When she didn't answer, Quentin grabbed her by the shoulder and spun the chair around.

"What's the matter, are you deaf?"

His voice died in his throat. Never in their worst nightmare would any of the Bullock children have been able to imagine what would meet them in that old oaken rocker. Nor would they ever forget, until the day they died, the ghastly face of death grinning at them.

The skin on the corpse's face, what was still attached to the skull, had shriveled to a purplish gray. The rest was dry as paper. One eye was missing from its socket. The other, looking like a shriveled Ping-Pong ball, hung by a slender strand of skin against the bony cheek next to the spot where her nose had been.

If the body had just been mummified it might have been easier to bear. But it was clear the corpse had been ravaged by insects and rodents before it dried and shriveled in the light of the broken window.

This was all that remained of Ariadne Belljar. And in the terrible, brief moment before Elliot howled with fright and Muffie gagged uncontrollably and Quentin dropped the candle in shock, they all realized that not only was Ariadne dead, but she must have been dead for almost forty years!

13

Suddenly, the flame of Elliot's candle caught the hem of Ariadne's skirt and the mummy went up like a torch.

"Oh, my God!" Quentin shrieked. "She's on fire."

Elliot, who was gasping for air in between hysterical screams, fled out of the attic and down the stairs, followed closely by Muffie. Her screams of terror had turned into pathetic sobs. She kept repeating, "Mommy! Daddy! Help us, please."

"Fire!" Quentin bellowed as he raced out of the attic. He scrambled down the stairs and lunged for the phone in the foyer. "Dial 911! Dial 911!"

Muffie and Elliot were already at the front door, trying to pry it open.

"Open the door. Oh, please, open the door," Muffie shouted at Elliot, who was tugging at the knob.

"I'm trying," he gasped. "But it's stuck."

"It can't be." Muffie wrapped her hands over

Elliot's fingers and pulled with all her might. The door still would not budge.

Quentin held the receiver up to his ear and shouted, "Help, there's a fire, come quickly — " He stopped short when he realized there was nothing but silence on the line. "The phone's dead," he said. "She must have cut the line." He was still holding the receiver close to his ear when a high-pitched laugh cackled across the dead phone line. He threw the telephone against the stairwell and screamed, "Let's get out of here!"

"The kitchen door," Elliot shouted. The three of them pounded across the living room and burst through the swinging door into the kitchen. Just as they did, they saw the door to the backyard swing shut and the dead bolt slide into place with a clang. Quentin pounded on the door with his fists, then tried to loosen the bolt but it was stuck fast.

"No escape," a voice whispered above the crackling flames that were rapidly consuming the upper floors of the old house.

"Did you hear that?" Muffie whimpered. "She won't let us go."

"That's right," the voice replied from right behind them.

The children spun around and saw the ghost of Ariadne Belljar, her umbrella tucked beneath her arm, the tapestry bag grasped in her left hand, hovering two feet above the dining room table. Before they could scream in fear, the image vanished, then reappeared in the kitchen, sitting on top of the stove.

"Now you're mine," the voice croaked from between lips that didn't move. "Forever."

The children fled into the living room, which was becoming choked with clouds of smoke.

"What are we going to do?" Muffie cried over and over again. "What can we do?"

"We'll get out through a window." Quentin coughed, covering his mouth with his hand. The smoke was stinging his eyes and tears were streaming down his cheeks.

Elliot tugged at the handles of the bay windows but they came off in his hands. "It's no good," he shouted.

Quentin saw the marble flower vase and, picking it up, he lifted it over his head, preparing to throw it through the glass.

"Don't fight me," she hissed. "I'm going to take care of you three — for all eternity. That's a promise."

Elliot crossed his fingers in front of him like a cross. "Leave me alone, you witch."

"Ha ha ha *ha!*"

The laughter rose to a deafening crescendo. To their horror, Ariadne's head lifted off her body and zoomed like a bullet toward Elliot. He dropped to the floor with a scream and lay flat against the wooden boards as it whooshed over him. "I didn't mean it," he mumbled. "Please don't hurt me, I didn't mean it."

Then the bony hands stretched out from the headless body, separated and flew across the room at Muffie, ready to ensnare her in their clutches. She turned and ran screaming to get away from them.

The gruesome head and hands chased Elliot and Muffie toward the stairs, while the body turned and headed for Quentin. As it moved toward him, writhing snakes began to pour out of the holes where the head and hands had been. And snakes were the one thing Quentin loathed. He panicked and fled toward the stairwell where his brother and sister were already cornered.

He realized too late that that was just what the ghost of Ariadne Belljar wanted him to do. She had herded them like lambs to the slaughter, for there was nowhere left for them to run but up. The stairwell was already choked with thick smoke. On the second floor the fire burst through the closed doors with a roar, and orange flames licked at the walls of the corridor and began to roll mercilessly down the banister toward the children.

Quentin squeezed his eyes shut and forced himself not to think about the snakes. "Don't look at her," he shouted to Muffie and Elliot.

"I can't help it," Elliot moaned. "She's after me."

"She's just a ghost!" Quentin rasped. The smoke was choking his lungs and every time he tried to shout, he coughed. "A ghost, do you hear me! She only has power if we believe she's real — " He doubled over, racked with coughing.

Muffie could only whimper in reply as the hands clutched and grabbed at her clothes, forcing her up the stairs into the roaring flames.

"Forget about Ariadne," Quentin coughed. "It's the fire that's the real danger. We haven't much time."

"Your time has run out, my little friend." Ariadne's voice was a wheeze over the crackling, spitting furnace looming above their heads. "Soon you'll be mine forever!"

Quentin fought off another coughing spasm and, gathering all of his strength, shouted, "Never!"

The horrible mocking laughter echoed through the house. It seemed to be coming from all around them.

Quentin suddenly spotted his worn leather bag on a table just on the other side of the stair railing. Inside that bag was his treasured taxidermy collection, soon to be lost forever. Suddenly his eyes widened and a ray of hope made his heart quicken. Inside that bag was — just possibly — the key to their escape.

"Elliot!" Quentin snatched up the bag and, pulling it open, groped inside until his fingers felt what he was looking for. "Catch!"

A brown fuzzy creature went flying through the air. Out of reflex Elliot stuck out his hand and snagged it in midair. "What is it?" he coughed.

"Selsdon," Quentin cried with glee.

"Ugh!" Elliot held the big stuffed rat with the grimacing teeth out in front of him. To his surprise, the gnashing head of Ariadne somersaulted backwards away from him. "She's still afraid of rodents!" Elliot shouted.

"Muffie," Quentin shouted at his sister.

The little girl had practically given up. She was huddled against the steps in a tight fetal position, only moving when the hands poked or prodded her.

"Muffie, stop crying and take this!" Quentin staggered forward and shoved a petrified bat into his sister's hand. She whimpered and held it out to the hands like an offering. The hands snatched the bat with a fury, then pulled back as if they'd been burned.

"It's working," Quentin tried to cheer but he was racked by another coughing fit. While he was bent over, he noticed the pile of folded sheets that were used to cover the furniture. They still rested on the chair by the archway into the living room. Thinking quickly, he ran over, picked them up, and rushed back to join his brother and sister. Wrapping himself in a top sheet, he tossed the others to Muffie and Elliot and ordered, "Put these on."

"What — ?" Elliot started to protest but Quentin roared, "Just *do* it!"

Suddenly a deafening explosion rocked the house and Muffie shouted, "What was that?"

"The fire must have reached the gas line for the

hot water heater in the upstairs bathroom," Quentin guessed.

"We've got to get out of here," Elliot groaned. "Now."

"You're mine!" Ariadne's voice hissed. "I'll never let you go. Never!"

"Into the dining room," Quentin shouted as he shoved and pushed Muffie and Elliot out of the smoke-clogged living room. "We'll break out through the French windows."

"Over my dead body!" Ariadne's voice cackled. To the children's chagrin, the body parts that had been floating around the room reassembled themselves in front of the French windows, blocking their escape.

"We're trapped!" Muffie sobbed. "She'll never let us leave."

"Selsdon!" Quentin rasped. "Throw Selsdon at her."

Elliot squinted down at the grotesque stuffed animal. "Why do I have to throw mine?" he demanded. "You throw yours!"

"Has your brain melted?" Quentin snapped. "Throw it!"

"Quentin!" Muffie shrieked as the ceiling in the room behind them bowed and sagged with a horrendous groan. "The roof's caving in."

A flaming timber broke through and crashed onto the floor.

"Give me that!" Quentin yanked the rat out of his brother's grasp and heaved it with all his might

126

at the looming figure of Ariadne Belljar. With a shriek her body split into several different parts and Quentin shouted, "Now!"

"Now?" Muffie repeated.

Quentin didn't waste any more breath. Instead he tightened his sheet over his head and, grabbing his sister and brother by the hand, ran for the French windows and leapt.

14

The sun was just setting when the Bullocks pulled into the driveway of Maldemere. They were greeted by the sight of the biggest bonfire they had ever seen in their lives. The old mansion was completely ablaze, a boiling column of smoke curling up into the pink sky.

"The children!" Mrs. Bullock screamed. Then she promptly fainted, bumping her head against the dashboard.

If she had waited just a fraction of a second longer before passing out, Mrs. Bullock would have seen three figures draped in white burst through the French windows of the dining room.

The children had tumbled onto the grass and rolled down the slight incline onto the safety of the gravel drive. Muffie suffered a scraped elbow, Elliot a bruised knee, and Quentin's glasses were snapped in two. Otherwise, they were unharmed.

After a long night filled with fire engines and endless interrogations by the police, the Bullocks were now preparing to leave Bar Harbor. They had spent the night in a motel and eaten breakfast at McDonalds.

"I don't care if Father does ground us for life," Elliot said, taking a bite of his Egg McMuffin. The children were waiting in the van for their parents to finish signing some papers at the real estate office. "At least Ariadne's gone."

"Are you sure she won't come back?" Muffie asked, peering nervously out of the van windows at the streets of Bar Harbor.

"How could she?" Quentin poked at the bridge of his glasses, where the fireman had repaired them with silver duct tape. "You saw how the house collapsed like an accordion. I mean, the second floor fell into the first and then the whole thing dropped into the cellar. It was a complete and total meltdown."

"And remember the sound?" Elliot said, swallowing his food with a loud gulp. "That weird, high-pitched wail?"

Quentin nodded. "That had to be Ariadne's ghost finally disappearing."

"I'm glad she's gone," Muffie said, taking a sip of her hot chocolate. "But I can't help feeling a teensy bit sorry for her."

"Sorry for her!" Elliot nearly choked on one of the fries he'd stolen from Quentin's carton. "That old hag! How could you feel sorry for her?"

"Ariadne didn't stay in that house all those years because she wanted to. She stayed because the Kensingtons locked her in the attic. The police said so." Muffie shuddered. "It must have been terrible for her."

Quentin nodded. "No wonder she hated rats and bats—she must have had to eat them."

"Yeah," Elliot said. "And then they ate her."

"Oooh gross!" Muffie squealed.

"It's a good thing the judge is dead," Quentin added, "or he would probably be up on charges of murder."

Elliot shook his head. "I bet not. I bet Ariadne was tormenting that family, too, and the only way to keep her away was to shove her in the attic, lock the door, and go into hiding."

Quentin squinted one eye shut. "You've got a point there. Otherwise, why would they have left so fast, unless they were running from something? They must have thought their lives were in danger."

Elliot successfully stole a handful of his brother's fries and popped them in his mouth. "Then they weren't hiding from the police," he mumbled. "They were hiding from Ariadne."

Muffie started to open the sliding van door. "Should we go tell Mother and Father our theory?"

"Then they'd have to tell the police and we'd have to stay in this town a few more hours," Quentin warned, putting his hand on her arm. "I say the sooner we get out of here, the better."

"You're right." Muffie sat back in her seat. "We'll just keep quiet."

There was a sudden commotion on the sidewalk next to the van and the children watched their father shake hands with the real estate agent, the policeman, and the local fire chief. "Sorry for all of this trouble," Mr. Bullock said in his booming voice. "If the insurance company has any more questions, just have them call me."

Mrs. Bullock stood beside him, nervously tucking a strand of her hair behind one ear. "I don't know what possessed them to play with matches," she murmured apologetically. "We've warned them about that time and time again."

"Let's face it, Jenny," Mr. Bullock sighed, running his hand through his hair. He was wearing the clothes he had worn the night before, only they were rumpled and blackened from the smoke. "They're out of control. Which is why a trip to their grandmother's is just the thing."

The children listened to the conversation and Elliot muttered, "I don't know why you told them we were playing with matches, Quentin. I think we should have stuck by the truth."

"We tried that," Quentin said. "And they didn't buy it. Three hours of interrogation and — "

"You just cracked," Muffie cut in. She patted her brother on the arm. "It's understandable."

Quentin smiled at his sister. That was one good thing that had come out of their terrible adventure. The three of them were actually becoming friends.

"All right, children, fasten your seat belts," Mr.

Bullock said as he climbed wearily into the van. "We're off to your grandmother's."

"What are you and Mother going to do while we're in Connecticut?" Muffie asked as the van pulled away from the curb. They wound their way through the tiny town of Bar Harbor, circling the town square that was already filled with tourists.

Her father smiled, his first smile since the day before. "Your mother and I have decided to take a little cruise up to Nova Scotia. We've had our family time together. Although it was short, it was action-packed, and now we think we need a little R and R."

Their father made a right turn onto the highway leading out of town.

"Good-bye, Bar Harbor!" Elliot called as he thumbed his nose out the rear window at the town.

"Good-bye, Maldemere!" Quentin and Muffie chorused as they passed the road to the now burnt-out shell of a house.

"And good-bye — " All three children lowered their voices so their parents wouldn't hear and whispered, "Ariadne."

Mrs. Bullock turned to look over the seat at the children. "Our first stop is the L.L. Bean outlet to buy some new clothes, and then we'll be on our way to your grandmother's house."

"Didn't anything survive the fire?" Muffie asked, thinking of all the beautiful dresses she had so carefully arranged in her closet.

Mr. Bullock nodded. "A couple of things. Quentin's bag — "

"But my collection was ruined," Quentin said mournfully. He pictured his rat Selsdon, and the mice and bats, all going up in flames. "Of course, I can always start a new one."

"Oh, goody." Mrs. Bullock smiled stiffly.

Muffie leaned forward in her seat. "What else did the fireman find in the fire?"

"Oh, let's see." Mr. Bullock scratched his head. "Elliot's rubber boots, a fishing hat of mine, and your mother's maroon tapestry bag."

Mrs. Bullock knit her eyebrows together. "What tapestry bag? I don't have a tapestry bag."

"Tapestry bag!" all three children gasped. "Where?"

Mr. Bullock gestured with his thumb over his shoulder. "I tossed it in the back. It's really amazing, too. It doesn't seem to have been touched by the fire. Oh, there was a blue umbrella with it."

Quentin's, Muffie's and Elliot's eyes nearly popped out of their heads. But none of them had the courage to turn and look in the seat behind them. They sat paralyzed, feeling as if giant spiders were crawling up their spines.

"You don't think . . . ?" Elliot murmured.

"It couldn't be," Quentin moaned.

"Oh, please don't let it be true!" Muffie whimpered.

Mr. Bullock reached up to adjust the rearview

mirror and that's when the children saw her.

Ariadne was sitting in the seat behind them, her tapestry bag on her lap, the blue umbrella clutched firmly in her hands. A thin smile of triumph lit up her horrible face.

"Eternally Yours," she cackled. "And that's a promise."

About the Author

Jahnna N. Malcolm is really the pen name for the husband and wife team, Jahnna Beecham and Malcolm Hillgartner.

Jahnna and Malcolm hope they never have any brushes with the supernatural. Jahnna lived in a haunted old farmhouse in Ohio when she was a child and that was enough for her!

Together they have written over thirty-five books for kids, including the *Bad News Ballet* series for Scholastic, and the mystery series *Hart and Soul*. Jahnna and Malcolm currently live with their son Dash in an old log cabin on a lake in the northwestern corner of Montana . . . a perfect spot for ghostly appearances.

If chilling out is your favorite thing to do, you'll love

GET
Goosebumps™
by R.L. Stine